William Shakespeare's King John: A Retelling in Prose

David Bruce

Published by David Bruce, 2022.

WILLIAM SHAKESPEARE'S KING JOHN: A RETELLING IN PROSE

First edition. July 26, 2022.

Copyright © 2022 David Bruce.

ISBN: 979-8201731564

Written by David Bruce.

Table of Contents

Dedication

DEDICATED TO MY SISTER MARTHA

Martha wrote, "When I was working at Longaberger, I worked with a girl who had two children and was in the middle of a divorce. She was so worried about Christmas for her boys. I received a very nice Christmas bonus that year, and I went to my boss and started a donation fund for the girl. My boss told me later that she — my boss —delivered the money to the girl's mother and father and told them not to tell her who brought the money for her. Months later the girl told me that the boys had the best Christmas that year, and she told me someone had brought money to her mom and dad for her, and she went to town and bought the boys Christmas. She never did know who did that for her. She was so thankful. I believe that I was the only one who donated to her, which was just fine."

***

The doing of good deeds is important. As a free person, you can choose to live your life as a good person or as a bad person. To be a good person, do good deeds. To be a bad person, do bad deeds. If you do good deeds, you will become good. If you do bad deeds, you will become bad. To become the person you want to be, act as if you already are that kind of person. Each of us chooses what kind of person we will become. To become a good person, do the things a good person does. To become a bad person, do the things a bad person does. The opportunity to take action to become the kind of person you want to be is yours.

Cover Image for William Shakespeare's *King John*: A Retelling in Prose:

King John. Licensed under Public Domain via Wikimedia Commons — http://commons.wikimedia.org/wiki/File:King_John.jpg#/media/File:King_John.jpg

Educate Yourself
Read Like A Wolf Eats
Be Excellent to Each Other
Books Then, Books Now, Books Forever

***

In this retelling, as in all my retellings, I have tried to make the work of literature accessible to modern readers who may lack the knowledge about mythology, religion, and history that the literary work's contemporary audience had.

Do you know a language other than English? If you do, I give you permission to translate this book, copyright your translation, publish or self-publish it, and keep all the royalties for yourself. (Do give me credit, of course, for the original retelling.)

I would like to see my retellings of classic literature used in schools, so I give permission to the country of Finland (and all other countries) to give copies of this book to all students forever. I also give permission to the state of Texas (and all other states) to give copies of this book to all students forever. I also give permission to all teachers to give copies of this book to all students forever.

Teachers need not actually teach my retellings. Teachers are welcome to give students copies of my eBooks as background material. For example, if they are teaching Homer's *Iliad* and *Odyssey*, teachers are welcome to give students copies of my *Virgil's* Aeneid: *A Retelling in Prose* and tell students, "Here's another ancient epic you may want to read in your spare time."

CAST OF CHARACTERS

Male Characters

King John of England.

Prince Henry, son to the King; after King John's death, he becomes King Henry III of England.

Arthur, Duke of Bretagne, nephew to the King; his father was King John's older brother Geoffrey.

Earl of Pembroke.

Earl of Essex.

Earl of Salisbury.

Lord Bigot.

Hubert de Burgh.

Robert Faulconbridge, son to Sir Robert Faulconbridge.

Philip, aka the Bastard, Robert Faulconbridge's half-brother; Philip's father is King Richard I of England, aka Richard the Lionheart. Philip's reputed father was Sir Robert Faulconbridge, and so early in life he was known as Philip Faulconbridge.

James Gurney, servant to Lady Faulconbridge.

Peter of Pomfret, a prophet.

Philip II, King of France.

Louis the Dauphin; after King Philip II's death (not in this book), he becomes King Louis VIII of France.

Lymoges, Duke of Austria.

Cardinal Pandulph, the Pope's legate.

Melun, a French Lord.

Chatillion, ambassador from France to King John.

Female Characters

Queen Eleanor, mother to King John; widow of King Henry II; she is also known as Eleanor of Aquitaine; her children include King Richard I, King John, and Geoffrey; one of her grandchildren is Blanche of Spain.

Constance, mother to Arthur; widow of Geoffrey, one of King John's older brothers.

Blanche of Spain, niece to King John; her grandfather is King Henry II of England and her grandmother is Queen Eleanor of England. One of Queen Eleanor's children is Eleanor of Castile; Blanche of Spain is her daughter. Blanche is also known as Blanche of Castile as well as Blanche of Spain. She marries Louis the Dauphin and later becomes Queen of France.

Lady Faulconbridge.

Minor Characters

Lords, Citizens of Angiers, Sheriff, Heralds, Officers, Soldiers, Messengers, and other Attendants.

Scene: England and France.

Nota Bene:

Between 1349 and 1830, "Dauphin" was the title given to the oldest living son of the King of France.

King John of England: 24 December 1166 to 19 October 1216. He reigned 6 April 1199 to 19 October 1216.

The King of England before King John was Richard I, known as Richard the Lionheart. He died without leaving behind legitimate children. Before dying, he wrote a will leaving the Kingship to his nephew Arthur, but on his deathbed Eleanor persuaded him to change his will and leave the Kingship to John, her son.

One conflict in this play is a disagreement about who is the legitimate King of England. Normally, the Kingship would pass to a legitimate son, but Richard the Lionheart had no legitimate son. Is the legitimate successor John, whom Richard the Lionheart named as his successor in his final will? Or is it Arthur, the son of a deceased older brother of John?

King Philip II of France: 21 August 1165 to 14 July 1223. He was Junior King from 1 November 1179 to 18 September 1180. He was Senior King from 18 September 1180 to 14 July 1223.

CHAPTER 1

— 1.1 —

King John of England, Queen Eleanor, the Earl of Pembroke, the Earl of Essex, and the Earl of Salisbury were in a room in King John's palace. With them were attendants and Chatillion, the ambassador from France to King John.

King John asked, "Now, tell us, Chatillion, what does the King of France want with us?"

"Thus, after greeting you, speaks the King of France in my person to the majesty, the borrowed majesty, of England here," Chatillion replied.

By referring to "borrowed majesty," he was saying that King John was not the true King of England.

Queen Eleanor said, "This is a strange beginning: 'borrowed majesty'!"

"Silence, good mother," King John said. "Listen to the message from the ambassador."

Chatillion continued, "King Philip II of France, in right and true behalf of your deceased older brother Geoffrey's son, Arthur Plantagenet, lays most lawful claim to this fair island and the territories, to Ireland, Poictiers, Anjou, Touraine, Maine. He commands you to lay aside the sword of state that rules usurpingly over these several lands, and put these lands into the hand of young Arthur, your nephew and the true royal sovereign of England."

"What happens if we don't do this?" King John asked, using the royal plural.

"The forceful compulsion of fierce and bloody war will enforce these rights so forcibly withheld," Chatillion replied. "If you won't willingly give these lands to Arthur, we will make war against you and force you to do so."

"Here we have war for war and blood for blood," King John said. "Compulsion will answer compulsion. This is my answer to the King of France."

"Then take my King's defiance from my mouth," Chatillion said. "This is the most extreme response permitted by my charge as ambassador."

"Bear my defiance back to him, and so depart in peace," King John said. "Be like lightning and appear before the eyes of the King of France, for before you can report your news I will be there, and the thunder of my cannon shall be heard. So leave! Be the trumpet of our wrath and be the sullen presentiment of your own destruction.

"Let him have an honorable escort. Pembroke, look to it.

"Farewell, Chatillion."

Chatillion and the Earl of Pembroke exited.

Queen Eleanor said, "What now, my son! Haven't I always said that ambitious Constance, the mother of Arthur, would not stop until she had kindled France and all the world to work toward the rights and on the side of her son? This might have been prevented and put right with very easy expressions of friendship, but now the rulers of two Kingdoms must arbitrate the matter with fearsome bloody consequences."

"On our side we have our strong possession of England and our right to be King," John said, using the royal plural.

Queen Eleanor whispered quietly to him, "Your strong possession of England is of much more worth than your right to be King. People will respect more your possession of the throne of England, or else it must go wrong with you and me. So much my conscience whispers in your ear, which none but Heaven and you and I shall hear."

A Sheriff entered the room.

Seeing him and knowing why he had come, the Earl of Essex said, "My liege, here is the strangest controversy that ever I heard come from country to be judged by you. Shall I produce the men?"

"Let them approach," King John said. "Our abbeys and our priories shall pay this expedition's expeditious charge — this sudden expense and speedy attack. They will pay for the war that I must fight."

Robert Faulconbridge and Philip Faulconbridge entered the room.

King John asked, "What men are you? Who are you?"

Philip Faulconbridge, who would quickly become informally known as the Bastard, said, "I am your faithful subject, a gentleman who was born in Northamptonshire and I am the eldest son, as I suppose, to Robert Faulconbridge, a soldier who was knighted in the field of combat by the honor-giving hand of Coeur-de-lion — Richard the Lionheart."

King John asked the other man, "Who are you?"

Robert Faulconbridge replied, "I am the son and heir to that same Faulconbridge."

"Is that man the elder son, and you are the heir?" King John said. "You came not of one mother then, it seems. You two men must have had different mothers."

Philip Faulconbridge said, "Most certainly one mother gave birth to both of us, mighty King. That is well known and completely certain, and, as I think, we had one and the same father. But for the certain knowledge of that truth, I direct you to Heaven and to my mother. I don't have certain knowledge of who is my father; all men's children lack that certain knowledge."

It is proverbial that men may know definitely who their mother is but not know definitely who their father is — at least in the days before DNA testing.

"Get out, rude man!" Queen Eleanor said. "You shame your mother and wound her honor with this distrust."

"I, madam?" Philip Faulconbridge said. "No, I have no reason for that distrust. That is my brother's plea and none of mine; my brother claims that I am illegitimate. And if he can prove that, he pops me out of my father's estate and takes away from me at least five hundred pounds a year. May Heaven guard my mother's honor and my land!"

"You are a good blunt fellow," King John said. "Why, being younger born, does he lay claim to your inheritance?"

"I don't know why, except to get the land," Philip Faulconbridge said. "But once he slandered me with bastardy. But whether I am as truly begotten as he or not, that still I lay upon my mother's head. But that I am as well begotten as he, my liege — may fair things befall the bones that took the pains for me! — compare my brother's and my faces and judge for yourself."

The two brothers did not look alike. Robert Faulconbridge was thin-faced and resembled his father: Sir Robert Faulconbridge. Philip Faulconbridge was a strongly built man and resembled the late King Richard I of England, aka Richard the Lionheart.

Philip Faulconbridge continued, "If old Sir Robert did beget us both and were our father and this son definitely resembles him, then oh, old Sir Robert, father, on my knee I give Heaven thanks I do not resemble you!"

King John said, "Why, what a madcap Heaven has lent us here! This man is a mad-brained fellow!"

"He has a trick of Coeur-de-lion's face and resembles him," Queen Eleanor said. "The accent of his tongue copies the accent of Richard the Lionheart's tongue. Don't you read some tokens of my son Richard the Lionheart in the large and powerful body of this man?"

Richard the Lionheart was one of King John's late brothers, and so King John knew well what he looked like.

"My eye has well examined this man's bodily parts and finds them to perfectly resemble Richard," King John said.

He then said to Robert Faulconbridge, "Sirrah, speak. What moves you to claim your brother's land?"

"Sirrah" was a term of address used when a person of high social status spoke to a male of lower social status.

Philip Faulconbridge interrupted and answered the question, "Because he has a half-face, like my father. With half that face he would have all my land: a half-faced groat worth five hundred pounds a year!"

A half-face is a thin face or a face shown in profile. A half-faced groat is a coin of little value.

Robert Faulconbridge said, "My gracious liege, when my father was still alive, your brother Richard the Lionheart much employed my father —"

Philip Faulconbridge interrupted, "Well, sir, by this you cannot get my land: Your tale must be how he employed my mother."

"Employed" meant "used the services of"; in this case, the term included the meaning "used the sexual services of."

Robert Faulconbridge continued, "And your brother once dispatched my father in an embassy to Germany so that he and the emperor there could treat of high affairs affecting that time.

"Your brother the King — Richard the Lionheart — took advantage of his absence and in the meantime sojourned at my father's home. How he prevailed there with my mother I am ashamed to say, but truth is truth. Large lengths of seas and shores between my father and my mother lay, as I have heard my father himself say, when this same robust gentleman — Philip Faulconbridge — was begotten. My father on his deathbed bequeathed in his will his lands to me, and he swore that this Philip Faulconbridge, my mother's son, was no son of his. And if he were, he came into the world fully fourteen weeks prematurely. So then, my good liege, let me have what is mine — my father's land, as was stated in my father's will."

In this society, a wife's child would be legally declared illegitimate if the husband was absent overseas for more than the entire nine months of the pregnancy; this had not happened in this case.

"Sirrah, your brother is legitimate," King John said. "Your father's wife bore him after wedlock, and if she played false, the fault was hers; this fault lies on the hazardous fortunes of all husbands who marry wives. This is a risk that all husbands take."

The word "fault" meant "sin"; it was also slang for "vulva."

King John continued, "Let us assume that it is true that my brother, as you say, took pains to get this son. What if he had from your father claimed this son for his? Truly, good friend, your father might have kept this calf bred from his cow from all the world. When a bull fathers a calf on a cow, the owner of the cow keeps the calf. Truly your father might; so then, if Philip Faulconbridge were my brother's son, my brother might not claim him, and your father, although Philip Faulconbridge is no child of his, could not refuse him. This concludes the matter. If the assumption we made is true, then my mother's son did beget your father's heir, and your father's heir must have your father's land."

King John was saying that the father's will did not count; what counted was legitimacy (or what is assumed to be legitimate). King Philip II of France would have agreed. King Richard I's will was not enough to make King John the true King of England. Since King Richard I had not left behind a legitimate son, what counted was being a legitimate son of the man who would have been next in line to be King if he were alive. Arthur was the legitimate son of Geoffrey, the man who if he had been alive would have been next in line to be King after Richard I.

Robert Faulconbridge said, "Shall then my father's will be of no force to dispossess that child who is not his? Doesn't my father's will count?"

Philip Faulconbridge interrupted, "Your father's will has no more force to dispossess me, sir, than was his will to beget me, as I think."

He was punning. "Will" meant three things: 1) intention, 2) sexual desire, and 3) penis.

Queen Eleanor asked Philip Faulconbridge, "Which would you rather be? Would you choose to be a Faulconbridge and be like your brother so you can enjoy your land? Or would you choose to be the reputed son of Coeur-de-lion,

Richard the Lionheart? If you choose to be known as his bastard son, you would be the lord of your presence and the lord of no land."

Philip Faulconbridge replied, "Madam, suppose my brother had my shape, and I had his shape, which is the shape of old Sir Robert, and suppose my legs were two such slender riding whips, my arms such stuffed eel-skins, and my face so thin that I would not dare stick a rose in my ear lest men should say 'Look, three-farthings is going there!'"

Three-farthing coins bore a profile of Queen Elizabeth I. Behind her ear was depicted a rose.

He continued, "And suppose his shape were heir to all this land, then I wish I might never stir from off this place. I would give away every foot of the land in order to have this face that I have. I would not be Sir Nob in any case."

"Nob" was a diminutive of "Robert." "Nob" also meant "knob" and "head."

Queen Eleanor said, "I like you well. Will you forsake your fortune, bequeath your land to your half-brother, Robert Faulconbridge, and follow me? I am a soldier and am now going to France to make war."

Philip Faulconbridge said, "Brother, you take my land, and I'll take my chances. Your face has gotten you five hundred pounds a year, yet if you were to sell your face for five pence, the price would be expensive because your face is not worth five pence.

"Madam, I'll follow you to the death."

Queen Eleanor joked, "No, I would have you go before me there."

Philip Faulconbridge joked, "Our rural manners give our betters way. Where I come from, the person with the higher rank goes first."

King John asked, "What is your name?"

Philip Faulconbridge, who had not yet stated his name, said now, "Philip, my liege, so is my name begun — Philip, good old Sir Robert Faulconbridge's wife's eldest son."

"From henceforth you will bear the name of the man whose form you bear," King John said. "You will change your name to Richard. Kneel down, Philip, but you will rise up a greater man."

Philip Faulconbridge knelt.

King John knighted him and said, "Arise, Sir Richard Plantagenet."

Plantagenet was the family name of Richard the Lionheart and of King John.

From now on, Philip Faulconbridge would be known as Sir Richard Plantagenet formally and as the Bastard informally. Sometimes he would be referred to as Philip or as Faulconbridge. Most often, as in this book henceforward, he would be called the Bastard.

The Bastard rose and said to Robert Faulconbridge, "Brother by the mother's side, give me your hand. My father gave me honor, yours gave you land. Now blessed be the hour, by night or day, when I was begotten, while Sir Robert was away!"

In this society, "hour" and "whore" were pronounced alike.

Queen Eleanor said, "This is the very spirit of Plantagenet! I am your grandmother, Richard; call me your grandmother."

"Madam, you are my grandmother by chance but not by truth," the Bastard said, "because my mother was not true and faithful to her husband. I am not your legitimate grandson. What of it, though?"

The Bastard now made several references to bastardy: "Something irregularly, a little from the right, in at the window, or else over the hatch."

Some doors were made of two half-doors: one above the other. The hatch is the lower half-door.

The Bastard continued, "Who dares not stir by day must walk by night, and have is have, however men catch and get hold of it. Near or far off, well won is still well shot."

Whether the archer is close to the target or far from it, a bull's-eye deserves praise. "Well-shot" also meant "well-ejaculated."

The Bastard continued, "And I am I, however I was begot."

King John said, "Go, Robert Faulconbridge. Now you have what you desired. A landless knight — the new Sir Richard Plantagenet — makes you a landed squire.

"Come, madam, and come, Richard, we must speedily go to France, for it is more than necessary that we go to France. Our need to go there is urgent."

The Bastard said to Robert Faulconbridge, "Brother, adieu. May good fortune come to you, for you were begotten in the way of honesty."

Everyone except the Bastard exited.

The Bastard spoke to himself about his new honors: "I am a foot of honor better than I was, but I am many and many foot of land the worse. Well, now can I make any common Joan a Lady.

"Someone will say to me, 'Good evening, Sir Richard!'

"I will reply, 'May God give you mercy, fellow!'

"And if his name is George, I'll call him Peter. For new-made men of honor forget men's names. People converted to a higher social rank find it too respectful and too sociable to remember the names of people of a lower social rank.

"Now I will be called 'your worship,' and I will invite a traveller — he and his toothpick — to dine with me."

Travellers sometimes used toothpicks — not then well known in England — as a way to show that they had travelled and were familiar with some of the ways that other cultures did things. A person such as the Bastard was not affected and chose to suck his teeth to remove food rather than use a toothpick. Despite being recently knighted, the Bastard had no intention of becoming affected; instead, he was mocking affectation.

The Bastard continued, "And when my knightly stomach is full, why then I will suck my teeth and catechize — question — my picked man of countries."

The traveller was picked because 1) he was refined and 2) he had picked his teeth with a toothpick.

The Bastard mocked polite conversation: "I will say, 'My dear sir.' Like this" — he demonstrated — "leaning on my elbow, I begin, 'I shall beseech you' — that is Question now, and then comes Answer like an Absey book."

An Absey book is an ABC book, or a primer, or a catechism book for children. Many such books were written in the form of questions and answers.

The Bastard continued, "'Oh, sir,' says Answer, 'at your best command. At your employment; at your service, sir.' 'No, sir,' says Question. 'I, sweet sir, am at yours.'

"And so, before Answer knows what Question wants to ask, except in dialogue of compliment, and talking about the Alps and the Apennines, the Pyrenees and the Po River, the end of suppertime draws near.

"But this is worshipful society and befits the mounting and ambitious spirit of a person such as myself. A person is but a bastard to the time — not a true child of the time — who does not smack — savor the taste — of the observation of polite courtesies. An ambitious person should be able to engage in polite conversation and formal dining.

"And I am a bastard, both a bastard in heritage and a bastard to the time —
whether I smack or not. I will be a bastard to the time whether or not I savor
the taste of the observation of polite courtesies. Even if I choose to engage in
polite social behavior, I will still be on the outside and not fully a member of
that culture.

"I will be a bastard and not a true child of the time not only in clothing and
device — my coat of arms would have a bar sinister to indicate my bastardy —
and not only in exterior form and outward special trappings, but also I will be a
bastard and not a true child of the time when it comes to the inward motion to
deliver sweet, sweet, sweet poisonous flattery for the age's tooth.

"Although I will not practice flattery to deceive others, yet to avoid being
deceived myself by flattery, I mean to learn about flattery because flattery shall
strew the footsteps of my rising. I am ambitious and intend to rise higher. I
know that others will flatter me in order to deceive me, but I have no intention
of being deceived in that way."

The Bastard looked up and saw a woman in riding clothes.

He said to himself, "But who comes in such haste in riding robes? What
woman-post is this? Has she no husband who will take pains to blow a horn
before her?"

Normally, men rode post horses, so seeing a woman-post was unusual.

People who rode post-horses rode quickly and so blew horns to warn
people to get out of their way. A horn also sounded to announce the post-rider's
arrival.

The Bastard made a joke when he said, "Has she no husband who will take
pains to blow a horn before her?" In stories about cuckolds, a husband who
blew his horn was publicly announcing that he was a cuckold. Cuckolds were
men with unfaithful wives; cuckolds were said to have invisible horns growing
on their heads.

Having dismounted, Lady Faulconbridge walked over to the Bastard.
Following her was James Gurney, her servant. Respectable women in this
culture would not travel without a male accompanying them.

The Bastard said to himself, "Oh, me! It is my mother."

He greeted her out loud, "How are you now, good lady! What brings you
here to court so hastily?"

"Where is that slave, your brother?" Lady Faulconbridge demanded. "Where is he, that man who pursues and hunts my honor up and down and everywhere?"

"Robert, my brother?" the Bastard asked. "Old Sir Robert's son? Colbrand the Giant, that same mighty man?"

Colbrand the Giant was the Bastard's mocking name for Robert Faulconbridge. In the fourteenth-century romance *Guy of Warwick*, the title character defeated Colbrand the Giant of Denmark.

The Bastard continued, "Is it Sir Robert's son that you seek so?"

"Sir Robert's son!" Lady Faulconbridge said. "Yes, you irreverent boy, Sir Robert's son. Why do you mock Sir Robert like that? He is Sir Robert's son, and so are you."

The Bastard said, "James Gurney, will you give us leave awhile?"

This was a polite request to be left alone with his mother. The Bastard's use of the servant's full and correct name showed that he was on familiar terms with the servants of his mother; it was also evidence that he would not allow his new knighthood to make him proud and affected.

"Good leave, good Philip," James Gurney replied.

The phrase "good leave" meant that yes, he would leave them alone.

"Philip!" the Bastard said. "Sparrow!"

Philip was his old name; it was a name commonly given to pet sparrows.

The Bastard said, "James, there's toys abroad. Soon I'll tell you more."

"Toys" are trifles. In this case, the toys were the Bastard's knighthood and new name. As you can see, the Bastard was not taking his new honors overly seriously.

James Gurney exited.

The Bastard said to his mother, Lady Faulconbridge, "Madam, I was not old Sir Robert's son. Sir Robert might have eaten his part in me on Good Friday and never broken his fast: He had no part in making me. Sir Robert could do well — I confess it — if he could beget me."

One meaning of the phrase "to do" is "to have sex."

The Bastard continued, "Sir Robert could not do it: He could not have begotten me. We know his handiwork: Look at his legitimate son Robert. Therefore, good mother, to whom am I beholden for these limbs? Sir Robert never helped to make this leg."

That Bastard's legs were muscular; Robert Faulconbridge's legs were scrawny.

Lady Faulconbridge asked, "Have you conspired with your brother, too? You should for your own gain defend my honor; that way, you will inherit the estate. What do you mean by this scorn, you most unmannerly knave?"

"Not knave — I am a knight, a knight, good mother, just like Basilisco," the Bastard replied.

Basilisco was a fictional character in Thomas Kyd's play *Soliman and Perseda* who insisted on being called a knight, not a knave.

The Bastard continued, "I have been dubbed a knight! I have it on my shoulder."

Part of the ceremony of making someone a knight involved tapping the man's shoulder with a sword.

The Bastard continued, "But, mother, I am not Sir Robert's son. I have disclaimed Sir Robert and my land. Legitimacy, name, and all are gone. So then, my good mother, let me know who is my father. Some proper man, I hope. Who was he, mother?"

"Have you denied that you are a Faulconbridge?" his mother asked.

"As faithfully as I deny the Devil," the Bastard replied.

"King Richard Coeur-de-lion was your father," Lady Faulconbridge admitted. "By a long and vehement suit, I was seduced into making room for him in my husband's bed. May Heaven not lay my transgression to my charge! You are the issue of — the child resulting from — my dear offence, which was so strongly urged past my defenses."

"Now, by this light, if I were to be begotten again, Madam, I would not wish for a better father," the Bastard said. "Some sins bear their privilege on Earth, and so does yours; your fault was not your folly."

Sins that bear their privilege on Earth are those that have immunity and advantages.

The Bastard continued, "You necessarily lay your heart at King Richard I's disposal; your heart was subjected tribute to commanding love, against whose fury and unmatched force the fearless lion could not wage the fight, nor keep his Princely heart from Richard's hand. He who by force robs lions of their hearts may easily win a woman's."

A legend about King Richard I stated that while he was being held prisoner, a lion was released in his cell to kill him. But when the lion roared, Richard thrust his naked hand and arm into the lion's throat and pulled out the lion's heart. This is how he came to be known as "Lionheart."

The Bastard continued, "Yes, my mother, with all my heart I thank you for my father! Anyone who lives and dares to say that you did not well when I was begotten, I'll send his soul to Hell. Come, lady, I will show you to my kin, and they shall say that when Richard begot me, if you had said no to him, it would have been a sin. Whoever says it was a sin, he lies; I say it was not."

The Bastard was cleverly punning on "not" and "naught." "Naught" has two meanings: 1) nothing, and 2) evil. In this culture, the word "naughty" had a much darker and more serious meaning than it does in our culture.

CHAPTER 2
— 2.1 —

Before the city of Angiers in France, two groups of people met. Angiers was a possession of England. In one group were the Duke of Austria and some of his forces, including drummers. In the other group were King Philip II of France and some of his forces. Also with him were Louis the Dauphin, his son, who was next in line to be King of France; Arthur, who had a claim to be King of England; Constance, Arthur's mother; and some attendants. The Duke of Austria was wearing a lion skin that he had taken from King Richard I — the Lionheart — of England.

Louis the Dauphin said, "We are well met before the city of Angiers, brave Duke of Austria.

"Arthur, that great forerunner of your blood, King Richard I, who robbed the lion of his heart and fought the holy wars — the Crusades — in Palestine, was sent by this brave Duke of Austria early to his grave. To make amends to his posterity, at our importuning he has come here to unfurl his battle flags, boy, in your behalf and to rebuke the usurpation of your unnatural uncle, John of England. Embrace him, love him, and give him welcome here."

Arthur said to the Duke of Austria, "God shall forgive you Coeur-de-lion's death all the sooner because you are giving life to his offspring, sheltering their right under your wings of war. I give you welcome with a powerless — lacking an army — hand, but with a heart full of unstained love."

Arthur then said, "Welcome before the gates of Angiers, Duke."

"You are a noble boy!" Louis the Dauphin said. "Who would not do right by you?"

The Duke of Austria kissed Arthur and said, "Upon your cheek I lay this zealous kiss as seal to this contract of my love. I swear that I will return no more to my home until Angiers and the territory you have rights to in France, together with that pale, white-faced shore, whose foot spurns back the ocean's roaring tides and defends from other lands her islanders, even until that England, hedged in with the ocean, that water-walled bulwark, always secure and confident — safe and sure — from foreign designs and plots, even until that utmost corner of the west salutes you as her King. Until you have all the land, including England, you have the right to possess, fair boy, I will not think of home, but instead will follow arms and the way of war."

Constance said, "Oh, take his mother's thanks, a widow's thanks, until your strong hand shall help to give him strength to make a better requital for your love and friendship!"

The Duke of Austria said, "The peace of Heaven is theirs who lift their swords in such a just and charitable war."

"Well then, let's get to work," King Philip II said. "Our cannon shall be aimed against the brows of this resisting town. Call for our men who best understand military strategy to select the spots that offer the best advantages for our cannon. We'll lay before this town our royal bones and wade to the marketplace in Frenchmen's blood, but we will make it subject to this boy."

"Stay for an answer to your embassy to King John," Constance advised, "lest unadvisedly and without proper deliberation you stain your swords with blood. My Lord Chatillion may bring from England that right in peace which here we urge in war, and then we shall repent each drop of blood that hot rash haste so unjustly and illegitimately shed."

Chatillion entered the scene.

Seeing him, King Philip II said, "It's a wonder, lady! Look, following upon your wish, our messenger Chatillion has arrived!

"Tell us briefly and quickly, gentle lord, what King John of England says. We calmly and coolly pause for you. Chatillion, speak."

"Then turn your forces from this paltry siege and stir them up against a mightier task," Chatillion replied. "King John of England, provoked by your just demands, has put himself in armor. The adverse winds, which kept me in England waiting for favorable winds, have given him time to land his legions here in France at the same time I landed here. His army marches quickly to this town. His forces are strong, his soldiers confident. Coming along with him is the Mother Queen. She is an Ate, a goddess of discord, stirring him to blood and strife. With her is her niece, the Lady Blanche of Spain. With them is a bastard of the deceased King Richard I, and all the unsettled humors — restless, disgruntled men — of the land. They are rash, inconsiderate, fiery volunteers, with ladies' faces and fierce dragons' spleens — that is, they are good-looking and have hot tempers. They have sold their fortunes at their native homes, and now bear their birthrights proudly on their backs in order to make hazard of new fortunes here; in other words, they sold all they had so they could equip themselves to make war against us. In brief, a braver choice of dauntless spirits than now the English ships have wafted over never has floated upon the swelling tide to do offence and scathing damage in Christendom."

The sound of King John's drums filled the air.

Chatillion continued, "The interruption of their churlish drums cuts off the telling of more details. They are at hand, either to parley or to fight; therefore, prepare yourselves."

"This expedition is very unexpected!" King Philip II said.

The Duke of Austria said, "By how much unexpected, by so much we must rouse our efforts for our defense, for courage rises when it is needed. Let them be welcome then; we are prepared."

King John, Queen Eleanor, Blanche, the Bastard, and some lords and forces arrived.

"May peace belong to France, if the King of France in peace permits our just and lineal entrance to our own town and territory," King John said. "If not, let France bleed, and let peace ascend to Heaven, while we, God's wrathful agent, punish the proud contempt of those who beat His peace and send it to Heaven."

King Philip II of France replied, "May peace belong to England, if your soldiers and their war return from France to England, there to live in peace. We love England, and it is for England's sake that we sweat here from the burden of our armor. This toil of ours should be your toil — you should be making sure that Arthur has his rights as the legitimate King of England. But you are so far from loving England that you have undermined England's lawful King. You have cut off the sequence of posterity, intimidated a child King, and raped the maidenly virtue of the crown.

"Look here upon your brother Geoffrey's face: Look at Arthur. These eyes, these brows, were molded out of his. Arthur is a child who is a little abstract — a little summary — of his father, Geoffrey, but with time he will become as huge a volume as his father.

"Geoffrey was born your elder brother, and this boy Arthur is his son; England was rightfully Geoffrey's and this boy is rightfully Geoffrey's, and so England is rightfully this boy's. In the name of God, how comes it then that you are called a King, when living blood beats in the temples of Arthur, who owns the crown that you have usurped?"

King John replied, "From whom have you received this great commission, King of France, that allows you to demand that I answer your charges — your articles of condemnation against me?"

King Philip II replied, "I have received my commission from that supernatural Judge Who stirs good thoughts in any breast of strong authority to look into the blots and stains affecting what is right: I have a commission to look into injustice. That Judge has made me guardian to this boy, Arthur, under whose warrant I charge you with injustice and with the Judge's help I mean to chastise it."

King John replied, "You usurp authority."

"I have an excuse," King Philip II said. "I usurp authority in order to beat down usurpation."

"Who is it you are calling a usurper, King of France?" Queen Eleanor asked.

"Let me make the answer," Constance, the mother of Arthur, said. "Your usurping son: John."

Eleanor and Constance were mother- and daughter-in-law. Eleanor had given birth to Richard the Lionheart, Geoffrey, and King John, and Constance was Geoffrey's widow.

"Damn you, insolent woman!" Queen Eleanor replied. "Your bastard shall be King so that you may be a Queen, and check the world!"

She was using the metaphor of a game of chess. A Queen can check — threaten — a King, and Blanche, if she were Queen, would check — threaten — the world.

"My bed was always to your son as true as your bed was to your husband," Constance said, "and this boy is more similar in his features to his father, Geoffrey, than you and John are in your manners and conduct, although you and John, your son, are as similar as rain is to water, or the Devil is to his dam. My boy a bastard! By my soul, I think his father never was so truly begotten. It cannot be, if you were his mother."

"There's a good mother, boy, who insults your father," Eleanor said to Arthur.

"There's a good grandmother, boy, who would insult you," Constance said to Arthur.

"Peace! Silence!" the Duke of Austria said.

"Hear the crier," the Bastard said.

In law courts, a crier cried, "Peace! Silence!"

"Who the Devil are you?" the Duke of Austria asked.

"One who will play the Devil, sir, with you," the Bastard said, "if he may catch your hide and you alone. You are the hare whose valor pulls the beards of dead lions, according to the proverb. I'll smoke your skin-coat — I'll beat you — if I catch you right. Sirrah, look to it; truly, I will, truly."

Blanche said, "Oh, well did he become that lion's robe who did disrobe the lion of that robe!"

The Duke of Austria was responsible for the death of Richard the Lionheart, who had owned the skin of the lion he had killed. Such skins could be worn as clothing. After the PanHellenic hero Hercules killed the Nemean Lion, he wore its skin. Now the Duke of Austria was wearing Richard the Lionheart's lion skin.

The Bastard said, "Richard's lion skin lies as attractively on the back of the Duke of Austria as great Alcides' shoes lie upon an ass."

"Alcides" is an alternate name of Hercules.

The Bastard was conflating two proverbial expressions: 1) Hercules' shoe will not fit a little foot, and 2) an ass in a lion's skin.

One of Aesop's fables is about an ass that found a lion skin and wore it. At first, the other animals were afraid when they saw the ass, but out of happiness at being feared, the ass brayed, and the other animals were no longer afraid of him. The proverb that came from the fable is this: "Fine clothes may disguise, but silly words will reveal a fool."

The Bastard's point was that the Duke of Austria was not the man that Richard the Lionheart was: He was like an ass compared to a lion.

The Bastard continued, "But, ass, I'll take that burden from your back, or lay on you a burden — blows — that shall make your shoulders crack."

The Duke of Austria asked, "What cracker — boaster — is this man who deafens our ears with this abundance of superfluous breath?

"King Philip, determine what we shall do immediately."

King Philip II said, "Women and fools, break off your conversation.

"King John, this is the very sum of all. I claim England and Ireland, Anjou, Touraine, and Maine as being the rightful possessions of Arthur; they do not belong to you. Will you resign them and lay down your arms?"

"I will as soon lay down my life," King John said. "I defy you, King of France.

"Arthur of Bretagne, yield yourself into my hand, and out of my dear love I'll give you more than the coward hand of France can ever win. Submit yourself to me, boy."

Queen Eleanor said to Arthur, "Come to your grandmother, child."

Constance used baby talk to say sarcastically to Arthur, "Do, child, go to its grandam, child. Give grandam Kingdom, and its grandam will give it a plum, a cherry, and a fig. There's a good grandam."

"To give someone the fig" meant "to make an insulting gesture at someone."

"My good mother, peace!" Arthur said. "I wish that I were laid low in my grave. I am not worth this disturbance that's made over me."

"His mother shames him so, poor boy," Queen Eleanor said. "He weeps."

"Now shame upon you, whether she does or not!" Constance said. "His grandmother's wrongs, and not his mother's shames, draw those Heaven-moving pearls — tears — from his poor eyes, which Heaven shall take in nature of a fee. Yes, with these crystal beads, which are like prayer beads, Heaven shall be bribed to do him justice and to do revenge on you."

"You monstrous slanderer of Heaven and Earth!" Queen Eleanor said.

"You monstrous injurer of Heaven and Earth!" Constance said. "Don't call me a slanderer. You and your son John usurp the dominions and the royal prerogatives and rights of this oppressed boy. This is your oldest grandson, and he is unfortunate in nothing except in you. Your sins are visited in this poor child: The canon of the law is laid on him, being but the second generation removed from your sin-conceiving womb."

Constance was referring to Exodus 20:5: "[...] *I the Lord thy God am a jealous God, visiting the iniquity of the fathers upon the children unto the third and fourth generation of them that hate me* [...]" (King James Version).

The canon of the law is the rule of the church.

"Madwoman, be quiet," King John ordered.

Constance replied, "I have only this to say, that he is not only plagued for her sin, but that God has made her sin and herself the plague on this grandson.

Eleanor committed adultery and gave birth to John, who is a bastard. Arthur is plagued because of her, and he is plagued by her. Her sin — the adultery that resulted in the birth of John — is her grandson's injury. Her injuriousness is the beadle — the officer who punishes sinners — to her sin. Both Eleanor and John are punishing Arthur, who ought not to be punished. The person who should be punished is Eleanor. All is punished in the person of this child, Arthur, and all is punished because of her — may a plague fall upon her!"

"You rash, foolhardy scold," Queen Eleanor said, "I can produce a will that bars the title of your son."

Richard the Lionheart had made a will that declared John would inherit his throne.

In her reply, Constance used the word "will" to mean "desire" and "sexual desire."

She said, "True, who doubts that? A will! A wicked will. A woman's will; a cankered, diseased grandmother's will!"

"Peace, lady, quiet!" King John ordered. "Pause, or be more calm and temperate. It ill beseems this presence to cry 'Aim!' to these ill-tuned repetitions. It is not fitting for this royal company to encourage these harsh-sounding accusations."

Spectators to an archery match cried "Aim!" as a way to encourage an archer.

King John ordered, "Let some trumpeter summon hither to the walls these men of Angiers. Let us hear them say whose title they permit: Arthur's or John's. They will tell us whether they believe Arthur is King of England, or I am."

The trumpet sounded. Some citizens appeared on the wall of the city.

The first citizen asked, "Who is it who has summoned us to the walls?"

King Philip II said, "It is the King of France, on behalf of Arthur, King of England."

King John said, "It is the King of England, on behalf of himself. You men of Angiers, and my loving subjects —"

King Philip II interrupted, "You loving men of Angiers, Arthur's subjects, our trumpet called you to this gentle parley —"

Using the royal plural, King John interrupted, "— for our benefit; therefore, listen to us first.

"These flags of France that are advanced here before the eye and prospect of your town have marched here to your harm. The cannons have their bowels full of wrath, and they are ready mounted to spit forth their iron indignation against your walls. All preparation for a bloody siege all mercilessly proceeding from these French soldiers confronts your city's eyes, your winking — opening and closing — gates. And except for our approach, those sleeping stones, which like a belt girdle you and make up your city walls, would have been attacked. The French army's ordinance would have compelled the stones of your city wall to leave their fixed beds of mortar, and wide havoc that is made for bloody power would have rushed upon your peace."

The cry "havoc!" to soldiers meant "attack and pillage and show no mercy!"

King John continued, "But at the sight of us, your lawful King, who diligently with much expeditious marching have brought a countercheck — a counter maneuver — before your gates, to save unscratched your city's threatened cheeks, behold, the dumbfounded French permit a parley.

"And now, instead of cannonballs wrapped in fire that would make a shaking fever in your walls, they shoot only calm words folded up in smoke — deceitful and obscure words. They want your ears to make an error and trust words that are not backed up by faith.

"Kind citizens, trust their words as they ought to be trusted, and let in your city us, your King, whose labored spirits, wearied in this action of swift speed, craves harborage and shelter within your city walls."

King Philip II said, "When I have finished talking, make answer to us both."

He took Arthur's hand in his right hand and said, "Look, in this right hand, whose protection is most divinely vowed to support the just rights of him whose hand it holds, stands young Arthur Plantagenet, son to the elder brother of this man named John, and King over him and all that he enjoys.

"For that which is right but has been downtrodden and oppressed, we tread in warlike march these greens before your town, but we are no further enemy to you than the constraint of hospitable zeal in the relief of this oppressed child religiously provokes.

"Be pleased then to pay that duty that you truly owe to that boy who owns it, namely this young Prince, and then our arms, just like a muzzled bear except in appearance, will end all offence. Our cannons' malice shall vainly be spent against the invulnerable clouds of Heaven, and with a blessed and unmolested retreat, with unhacked swords and helmets all unbruised by blows, we will bear home again that fierce energy and blood that we came here to spout against your town. And so we will leave your children, wives, and you in peace.

"But if you foolishly ignore our proffered offer, the round circumference of your walls that are so well built that they did not require refacing cannot hide you from our messengers of war — our cannonballs — even if all these English and their military discipline were harbored in your wall's rough circumference.

"Then tell us, shall your city call us lord, on behalf of Arthur, on whose behalf we have challenged your city? Or shall we give the signal to release our rage and martial spirit and stalk in blood to our possession? Shall we attack your city and through warfare gain possession of it?"

The first citizen replied, "In brief, we are the King of England's subjects. For him, and in his right, we hold this town."

"In his right" meant "in his rightful ownership."

"Acknowledge then the King, and let me in," King John said.

The first citizen replied, "We cannot do that, but he who proves himself to be the King, to him we will prove loyal. Until that time we have closed our gates against the world."

King John asked, "Doesn't possession of the crown of England prove who is the King? And if that doesn't, I bring you witnesses, twice fifteen thousand hearts of England's breeding —"

The Bastard said, "Bastards, and otherwise."

King John continued, "— to verify our title with their lives."

King Philip II said, "As many and as well-born bloods as those —"

The Bastard said, "Including some bastards."

King Philip II continued, "— stand in his face to contradict his claim."

The first citizen responded, "Until you settle whose right is worthiest, we on behalf of the worthiest withhold the right from both of you."

King John said, "Then may God forgive the sin of all those souls who to their everlasting residence, before the dew of evening falls, shall fleetly flee from this mortal world in dreadful battle to determine our Kingdom's King!"

"Amen! Amen!" King Philip II said. "Mount, chevaliers! To arms!"

Chevaliers are French knights.

The Bastard said, "Saint George, who thrashed the dragon, and ever since sits on his horseback at my hostess' door, teach us some fencing and some defense!"

Saint George, the patron saint of England, appeared mounted on horseback on the signs of many English inns.

The Bastard then said to the Duke of Austria, "Sirrah, if I were at your home, at your den, with your lioness I would set an ox-head onto your lion's hide, and make a monster of you."

Lionesses had the reputation of especially liking sex. The Bastard was saying that he would give the Duke of Austria horns by sleeping with his wife and making him a cuckold.

"Peace! Silence! Say no more," the Duke of Austria said.

"Oh, tremble, for you hear the lion roar," the Bastard said, sarcastically referring to the Duke of Austria, who was wearing Richard the Lionheart's lion skin.

"Let's go up higher to the plain," King John ordered, "where we'll set forth in the best arrangement all our regiments."

The Bastard said, "Let us hurry, then, to take the most advantageous place of the battlefield."

King Philip II said, "It shall be so, and at the other hill command the rest to stand. Fight for God and our right!"

The two Kings set their troops in military formation and then the battle began.

After the battle was over, a French herald, with trumpeters, went to the gates of the city and said, "You men of Angiers, open wide your gates, and let young Arthur, Duke of Bretagne, in, who by the help of the King of France this day has made much reason for tears in many English mothers whose sons lie scattered on the bleeding ground. Many a widow's husband lies prostrate, coldly embracing the discolored earth, and victory, with little loss, plays upon the dancing banners of the French, who are at hand, triumphantly displayed in formation, and are prepared to enter your city as conquerors and to proclaim Arthur of Bretagne England's King and yours."

The English herald then arrived, accompanied by trumpeters, and said, "Rejoice, you men of Angiers, ring your bells. King John, your King and England's, approaches. He is commander of this hot malicious day. The English armored soldiers, who marched here so silver-bright, hither return all gilt with the blood of Frenchmen. No plume stuck in any English crest has been removed by a French spear shaft. Our colors return in those same hands that displayed them unfurled when we first marched forth, and, like a troop of jolly huntsmen, come our vigorous, strong English soldiers, all with purpled hands, dyed in the dying slaughter of their foes."

In this culture, hunters dipped their hands in the blood of the deer they had killed.

The English herald continued, "Open your gates and give the victors entry."

The first citizen said, "Heralds, from off our towers we have beheld, from first to last, the onset and retire of both your armies, whose equality by our best eyes cannot be criticized. Your two armies have fought to a standstill. Blood has bought blood, and blows have answered blows. Strength has matched with strength, and power has confronted power. Both sides are alike, and both alike we like. One side must prove greater. While both sides weigh so evenly, we hold our town for neither, yet for both."

King John and King Philip II arrived, along with many soldiers.

King John spoke to the King of France, using a metaphor. He imagined his right to the throne as a current that was being blocked by the impediment of the King of France. Irritated by the impediment, his right to the throne would spill over the banks and flood the surrounding area, causing destruction.

King John said, "King of France, do you still have more blood to cast away? Tell me whether the current of our right shall run on? Our current's passage, vexed with your impediment, shall leave its native channel and overswell with a disturbed course even your confining shores, unless you let its silver water keep a peaceful progress to the ocean."

King Philip II replied, "England, you have not saved one drop of blood in this hot trial more than we of France have; instead, you have lost more blood than we have. And by this hand that holds sway over the earth this part of the sky overlooks, I swear before we will lay down our just-borne — justly borne and just-now borne — arms, we'll put down you, against whom these arms we bear, or add a royal number and name to the list of the dead, gracing the scroll that tells of this war's loss with slaughter coupled to the name of Kings."

In other words, one or the other King would die on the battlefield.

"Majesty! Ha!" the Bastard said. "How high your glory towers, when the rich blood of Kings is set on fire! Oh, now Death lines his dead jaws with steel. The swords of soldiers are his teeth, his fangs. And now Death feasts, mousing — tearing — the flesh of men, in unresolved quarrels of Kings. Why do these royal faces stand amazed and thunderstruck like this? Kings, cry 'Havoc!' Go back to the bloodstained battlefield, you equal potentates, you fiery kindled spirits! Then let the destruction of one side confirm the other's peace. Until then, blows, blood, and death!"

"Whose side do the townsmen yet admit to be King of England and admit into the town?" King John asked.

"Speak, citizens, for England," King Philip II said. "Who's your King?"

"The King of England," the first citizen said, "when we know who is the King."

Using the royal plural, King Philip II said, "Know him in us, who here uphold his rights."

Using the royal plural, King John said, "Know him in us, who are our own great deputy and bear possession of our person here, lord of our presence, of Angiers, and of you."

King John was pointing out that unlike Arthur, he needed no deputy to act for him.

"A greater power than we denies all this," the first citizen said.

This society believed in trial by combat: God would help the victor, and so the victor was in the right. These two armies, however, had fought to a standstill with no clear victor.

The first citizen continued, "And until who is King of England is beyond doubt, we lock our former doubt about the right thing to do in our strong-barred gates, Kings of our fears, until our fears, resolved and allayed, be by some certainly legitimate King purged and deposed."

The Bastard said, "By Heaven, these scoundrels of Angiers flout you and mock you, Kings. They stand securely and safely on their battlements, as if they were in a theater, from whence they stare and point at your industrious and laborious scenes and acts of death.

"Allow your royal presences to be ruled by me. Do like the mutineers of Jerusalem did. Be friends for a while and both of you join together and aim your sharpest deeds of malice on this town. By east and west let the King of

France and the King of England mount their battering cannon charged to the mouths, until the cannons' soul-frightening clamors have brawled down the flinty ribs of this contemptuous city. I'd aim the cannon incessantly upon these jades — these worthless wretches — even until unfenced desolation leaves them as naked as the common air.

"Once that is done, separate your united strengths, and part your mingled battle flags once again. Turn face to face and bloody spear point to bloody spear point. Then, in a moment, Fortune shall cull forth out of one side her happy favorite, to whom in favor she shall give the day, and kiss him with a glorious victory.

"How do you like this wild counsel, mighty heads of state? Doesn't it smack something of political intrigue?"

King John replied, "Now, by the sky that hangs above our heads, I like it well. King of France, shall we knit our armies together and lay this Angiers even to the ground, and then afterward fight over who shall be King of it?"

The Bastard said to King Philip II, "If you have the mettle of a King, being wronged as we are by this peevish town, then turn the mouth of your artillery, as we will ours, against these insolent walls, and when we have dashed them to the ground, why then we will defy each other and pell-mell we will make battle upon each other, sending souls either to Heaven or Hell."

"Let it be so," King Philip II decided.

He asked King John, "Tell me, from where will you assault the city?"

King John replied, "We from the west will send destruction into this city's bosom."

"I will send destruction from the north," the Duke of Austria said.

King Philip II said, "Our thundering cannon from the south shall rain their drift of cannonballs on this town."

The Bastard said to himself, "Oh, prudent military discipline! From north to south, the Duke of Austria and the King of France will shoot in each other's mouth. I'll encourage them to do it."

He said out loud, "Come, away, away! Let's go!"

The first citizen of Angiers said, "Listen to us, great Kings. Please wait a while, and I shall show you peace and a fair-faced alliance and treaty. You will win this city without a sword stroke or a wound. You will rescue those breathing lives who come here as sacrifices for the battlefield; you will rescue them so that they can die in beds. Don't persevere in destroying the city, but listen to me, mighty Kings."

King John said, "Speak on with permission; we are inclined to hear what you have to say."

The first citizen said, "That daughter there of Spain, the Lady Blanche, is the niece of King John of England. Look upon the years of Louis the Dauphin and that lovely maiden. If lusty love should go in quest of beauty, where would he find it fairer than in Blanche? If zealous love — holy love — should go in search of virtue, where would he find it purer than in Blanche? If ambitious love should seek a match of birth — a dynastic marriage — whose veins enclose richer blood than those of Lady Blanche?

"Such as she is, in beauty, virtue, and birth, so also is the young Dauphin in every way complete. If he is not complete in anything, say he is not she. And she again falls short of nothing, and so lacks nothing, except that she is not he.

"This man and this woman each requires the other to make their own perfection more perfect.

"He is the half part of a blessed man, left to be finished by such as she. And she is a fair divided excellence, whose fullness of perfection lies in him."

"Oh, two such silver currents, when they join, glorify the banks that bound them in, and two such shores to two such streams made one, two such controlling bounds shall you be, Kings, to this Prince and Princess, if you marry them to each other.

"This union shall do more than the battery of cannonballs can to open our fast-closed gates, for at this match, with swifter eagerness than gunpowder can enforce, the mouth of passage — our city gate — we shall fling wide open, and give you entrance to our city.

"But without this marriage match, the enraged sea is not half so deaf, lions more confident, mountains and rocks more free from motion, no, not Death himself in moral fury half so peremptory, as we are to keep this city."

The Bastard said to himself, "Here's a stop that shakes the rotten carcass of old Death out of his rags! Here's a large mouth, indeed, that spits forth death and mountains, rocks, and seas, that talks as familiarly of roaring lions as maidens of thirteen do of puppy-dogs!

"What cannoneer begot this strong, vigorous, hot-blooded fellow? He speaks plain cannon fire, and smoke and explosive noise. He gives the bastinado

— the beating — with his tongue. Our ears are cudgeled. Not a word of his but buffets better than a fist of a soldier of France. Zounds! I was never so bethumped with words since I first called my brother's father Dad."

It's possible that the Bastard's brother's father knew that the Bastard was a bastard and so objected to being called Dad by him.

Queen Eleanor said to King John, "Son, listen to this proposed union and make this match. Give with our niece a dowry large enough to accomplish your goals: For by this marriage knot you shall so securely tie your now precarious assurance to the crown that yonder green, inexperienced boy shall have no Sun to ripen the bloom that promises a mighty fruit. His claim to be King of England shall never bear fruit."

Constance and Arthur were not present; they were in the French camp.

Queen Eleanor continued, "I see a yielding in the looks of the King of France. See how the French whisper. Urge them while their souls are capable of this ambition, lest zeal, now melted by the windy breath of soft petitions, pity, and remorse, cool and congeal again to what it was. Let the marriage take place before the French change their minds and renew their zeal to help Arthur."

The first citizen said, "Why don't the double majesties — the King of England and the King of France — answer our threatened town's friendly proposal for agreement?"

King Philip II said, "Let the King of England speak first. He has been eager to first speak to the citizens of this city."

He asked King John, "What do you have to say?"

King John replied, "If the Dauphin there, your Princely son, can in this book of beauty — Blanche — read 'I love,' her dowry shall weigh equal to that of a Queen: Anjou and fair Touraine, Maine, Poictiers, and all that we find liable to our crown and dignity upon this side of the English Channel, except this city now by us besieged, shall gild her bridal bed and make her rich in titles, honors, and promotions, as she in beauty, education, and blood holds hands with and is equal to any Princess of the world."

King Philip asked his son, "What do you say, boy? Look at the lady's face."

"I am, my lord," Louis the Dauphin said, "and in her eye I find a wonder, or a wondrous miracle: the shadow of myself formed in her eye. This shadow, being but the shadow of your son, becomes a Sun and makes your son a shadow."

In Blanche's eye Louis saw a reflection of himself. This reflection was a reflection of his Kingly father's royal, Sun-like glory. Therefore, it was fitting for the Sun — the King. It also made the son a shadow — something created by the Sun-like King.

The marriage was being made for dynastic purposes, and in marrying Blanche, Louis was merely an instrument being used to achieve the ambitions of his father.

Louis the Dauphin continued, "I protest I never loved myself until now infixed — captured and firmly held — I beheld myself drawn in the flattering tablet of her eye."

Although this would be an arranged marriage, Louis the Dauphin was not opposed to it. He loved the reflection of himself in Blanche's eye, and by extension he loved Blanche's eye and Blanche herself.

He then talked quietly to Blanche.

The Bastard talked to himself and made fun of Louis the Dauphin's use of language:

"'Drawn in the flattering tablet of her eye!' Hanged, aka suspended, in the frowning wrinkle of her brow! And quartered, aka lodged, in her heart! He sees himself as a traitor in love. This is a pity now, that hanged and drawn and quartered, there should be in such a love so vile a lout as he."

In this culture, traitors to the King were hung, drawn, and quartered. They were hung but taken down from the rope while still alive. They then were disemboweled — their entrails were drawn out of their body. Finally, they were quartered — their bodies were cut into four pieces.

Blanche said to Louis the Dauphin, "My uncle's will and desire in this respect is mine. If he sees anything in you that makes him like you, then that anything he sees, which moves his liking, I can with ease translate it to my will — I can make it suit my own desires. Or if you prefer, to speak more properly, I will enforce it easily to my love.

"Further I will not flatter you, my lord, by saying that all I see in you is worthy of love, other than this: I see nothing in you, even if churlish thoughts themselves should be your judge, that I can find should merit any hate. I see nothing in you that I ought to hate."

King John said, "What say these young ones? What do you say, my niece?"

Blanche replied, "That she is bound in honor always to do what you in wisdom always deign to say."

"Speak then, Prince Dauphin," King John said. "Can you love this lady?"

"Ask me instead if I can refrain from loving her, for I do love her most unfeignedly," Louis the Dauphin replied.

"Then I give Volquessen, Touraine, Maine, Poictiers, and Anjou, these five provinces, with her to you," King John said, "and this in addition: fully thirty thousand marks of English coin.

"Philip of France, if you are pleased with this, command your son and future daughter-in-law to join hands."

"I like this well," King Philip II said. "Young Prince and Princess, join your hands."

"And your lips, too," the Duke of Austria said, "for I am well assured that I did so when I was first assured — that is, when I was first betrothed."

Louis the Dauphin and Blanche held hands and kissed.

The joining of hands and a kiss were enough for a legal marriage, but a church wedding customarily followed.

King Philip II said, "Now, citizens of Angiers, open your gates. Let in that amity that you have made, for at Saint Mary's chapel immediately the rites of marriage shall be solemnized.

"Isn't the Lady Constance in this troop? I know she isn't, for her presence would have much interrupted this match we have made up. Where are she and her son? Tell me, whoever knows."

Louis the Dauphin said, "She is sad and impassioned at your highness' tent."

"And, by my faith, this league that we have made will give her sadness very little cure," King Philip II said.

"Brother of England, how may we content this widow lady? In her right we French came, but we, God knows, have turned another way, to our own advantage. We came to win the rights of Arthur, her son, but we have chosen to do something more advantageous to us."

"We will heal up all," King John said, "for we'll give young Arthur the titles of Duke of Bretagne and Earl of Richmond, and we will make him lord of this rich fair town."

He ordered, "Call the Lady Constance. Some speedy messenger, go to her and tell her to go to our solemnity: this marriage ceremony. I trust we shall, if not fill up the measure of her will, yet in some measure satisfy her so that we shall stop her exclamations of distress and outrage.

"Let us go, as well as haste will allow us, to this unlooked for and unplanned pomp."

Everyone except the Bastard exited.

The Bastard said to himself, "This is a mad world with mad Kings and a mad truce!

"John, to stop Arthur's title to the whole, has willingly parted with a part.

"And the King of France, whose conscience buckled on his armor, whom zeal and charity brought to the battlefield as God's own soldier, has been whispered to in the ear by that same purpose-changer, that sly Devil, that pimp who always breaks the head of faith, that daily vow-breaker, he who wins something from all — from Kings, beggars, old men, young men, and maidens, who, having no external thing to lose except the word 'maiden,' he cheats the poor maiden of that. To whom am I referring? I am referring to that smooth-faced, deceitful gentleman who is flattering self-interest — self-interest, the bias of the world.

"The world of itself is well balanced and made to run even upon even ground until this advantage, this vile-drawing bias, this sway of motion, this self-interest, makes it throw off the control of all impartiality and of all direction, purpose, course, and intent.

"And this same bias, this self-interest, this bawd, this pimp, this all-changing word, placed on the outward eye of ambition — as opposed to the inward eye of conscience — of the fickle King of France, has drawn him from his own determined aid, from a resolved and honorable war, to a most base and vilely concluded peace.

"And why do I rail against this self-interest? Only because self-interest has not wooed me yet. It's not because I have the power to clutch my hand shut when any fair angels — coins bearing the image of an angel — would salute my palm; instead, it's because the palms of my hands have not been tempted yet, and so like a poor beggar, I rail against the rich.

"Well, while I am a beggar, I will rail and say there is no sin except to be rich. And when I am rich, my virtue then shall be to say there is no vice except begging.

"Since Kings break faith when tempted by self-interest, then be my lord, Gain, for I will worship you."

The Bastard's words and actions did not match. Often he spoke cynically about following his own self-interest, but his deeds showed that he was loyal and patriotic.

CHAPTER 3

— 3.1 —

Constance, Arthur, and the Earl of Salisbury spoke together in the French King's pavilion. The Earl of Salisbury had brought Constance news about the marriage of Louis the Dauphin and Blanche, niece of King John.

Constance said to the Earl of Salisbury, "Gone to be married! Gone to swear a peace! False, faithless blood joined to false, faithless blood! Gone to be friends! Shall Louis have Blanche, and Blanche have those provinces?

"It is not so: You have misspoken; you have misheard. Be well advised and sensible; tell your tale again. It cannot be; you only say it is so.

"I trust I may not trust you, for your word is only the vain breath of a common man. Believe me: I do not believe you, man. I have a King's oath to the contrary. You shall be punished for thus frightening me, for I am sick and susceptible to fears, oppressed with wrongs and therefore full of fears. I am a widow, husbandless, subject to fears. I am a woman, by nature heir to fears.

"And even if you now confess you only jested, I cannot make peace with my vexed spirits, and they will quake and tremble all this day.

"What do you mean by shaking your head? Why do you look so sorrowfully at my son? What means that hand upon that breast of yours? Why does your eye hold that lamentable tear, like a proud river peering over its banks?

"Are these sad signs confirmers of your words? Then speak again; don't tell all your former tale, but say this one word: whether your tale is true."

The one word she wanted to hear was that his news was *not* true.

The Earl of Salisbury said, "My words are as true as I believe you think them — King Philip II and his son the Dauphin — false who give you reason to know that what I say is true."

Constance said, "Oh, if you teach me to believe this sorrow, then teach this sorrow how to make me die, and let belief and life encounter in the same way as does the fury of two desperate men who in their very meeting fall and die.

"Louis marry Blanche!"

She said to Arthur, "Oh, boy, then what will become of you and your claim on the throne of England?"

She continued, "With the King of France friends with the King of England, what becomes of me?

"Fellow, be gone: I cannot endure your sight. This news has made you a very ugly man."

Constance was so upset that she was speaking contemptuously to the Earl of Salisbury, including calling him "fellow."

The Earl of Salisbury replied, "What other harm have I, good lady, done, except speak the harm that is by others done?"

"Which harm within itself is so heinous that it makes harmful all who speak of it," Constance said.

"I beg you, madam, be calm," Arthur said.

"If you, who bid me to be calm, were grim, ugly, and slanderous to your mother's womb, full of unpleasing blots and sightless stains, lame, foolish, crooked, swarthy, monstrous, patched with foul moles and eye-offending marks, I would not care, I then would be calm, for then I should not love you, no, nor would you become and suit your great birth nor would you deserve a crown.

"But you are good-looking, and at your birth, dear boy, Nature and Fortune joined to make you great. Of Nature's gifts you may with lilies boast, and with the partially blossomed rose."

The lily is a symbol of France, and the rose is a symbol of England.

Constance continued, "But Fortune, oh, she is corrupted, changed, and won from you. She commits adultery hourly with your uncle John, and with her golden hand has plucked on the King of France to tread down fair respect of sovereignty, and made his majesty the bawd to theirs. The King of France is a bawd to Fortune and to King John — that strumpet Fortune, that usurping John!"

She said to the Earl of Salisbury, "Tell me, fellow, isn't the King of France forsworn? Hasn't he broken his word? Poison him with words, or get you gone and leave those woes alone that I alone am bound to bear and endure and suffer."

"Pardon me, madam," the Earl of Salisbury said. "I may not go without you to the Kings."

"You may, you shall," Constance said. "I will not go with you. I will instruct my sorrows to be proud, for grief is proud and makes its owner stoop. To me and to the state of my great grief let Kings assemble, for my grief's so great that no supporter but the huge firm earth can hold it up. Here I and my sorrows sit. Here is my throne. Tell Kings to come bow to it."

She sat on the ground.

King John, King Philip II, Louis the Dauphin, Blanche, Queen Eleanor, the Bastard, the Duke of Austria, and some attendants walked over to her.

King Philip II said to Blanche, "It is true, fair daughter-in-law, and this blessed day always in France shall be kept a festival day. To solemnize this day, the glorious Sun stays in his course and plays the alchemist, turning with the splendor of his precious eye the meager cloddy Earth to glittering gold. The yearly course that brings this day about shall never see it except as a holiday."

Constance said, "It is a wicked day, and not a holy day!"

She stood up and said, "What has this day deserved? What has it done that it in golden letters to make it stand out should be set among the great festivals in the calendar? Instead, turn this day out of the week and delete this day of shame, oppression, and perjury.

"Or, if it must stand in the calendar, let pregnant wives pray that their children may not be born on this day, lest their hopes be disappointed with the birth of a monster. Let seamen fear shipwreck on no day except on this day. Let no agreements break except those that are on this day made. On this day, let all things begun come to an ill end. Yes, let faith itself change to hollow falsehood!"

"By Heaven, lady, you shall have no cause to curse the fair proceedings of this day," King Philip II said. "Haven't I pledged to you my majesty?"

Constance replied, "You have beguiled me with a counterfeit that merely resembles majesty, which, being tested and tried, proves to be valueless. You are forsworn, forsworn; you have broken your word. You came in arms to spill my enemies' blood, but now in arms — arm in arm with King John — you strengthen it with your blood. The grappling vigor and rough frown of war is cold in amity and feigned peace, and the oppression of Arthur and me has created the formation of this league.

"Arm, arm, you Heavens, against these perjured Kings! A widow cries; protect me as a husband would protect a wife, Heavens! Let not the hours of this ungodly day wear out the day in peace, but before sunset set armed discord between these perjured Kings! Hear me, oh, hear me!"

"Lady Constance, peace! Be calm!" the Duke of Austria said.

"War! War! No peace!" Constance shouted. "Peace is to me a war. Oh, Lymoges! Oh, Austria! You shame that bloody spoil — that lion skin taken from Richard the Lionheart. You slave, you wretch, you coward!

"You are little in bravery, but great in villainy. You are always strong upon the stronger side! You always choose to side with the stronger side! You are Lady Fortune's champion who never fights except when her temperamental ladyship is nearby to teach you how to keep yourself safe! You have perjured yourself, too, and you flatter great and powerful people. What a fool you are, a ramping, boasting fool, to brag and stamp and swear in my cause and on my side! You cold-blooded slave, haven't you spoken like thunder on my side, sworn that you are my soldier, told me that I can depend upon your stars, your fortune, and your strength, and do you now fall over to my foes?

"You wear a lion's hide! Take it off for shame, and hang a calfskin on those recreant limbs."

Lions are known for courageousness; calves are known for meekness.

"I wish that a man would speak those words to me!" the Duke of Austria said.

Immediately, the Bastard said, "And hang a calfskin on those recreant limbs."

"You dare not say so, villain, on your life," the Duke of Austria said.

Immediately, the Bastard repeated, "And hang a calfskin on those recreant limbs."

Using the royal plural, King John said, "We do not like this; you forget your place."

Cardinal Pandulph arrived.

Seeing him, King John said, "Here comes the holy legate of the Pope."

"Hail, you anointed deputies of Heaven!" Cardinal Pandulph said. "To you, King John, my holy errand is. I, Pandulph, Cardinal of fair Milan, and from Pope Innocent III the legate here, do in his name religiously demand why you against the church, our holy mother, so willfully spurn, and with violent compulsion keep Stephen Langton, whom the Pope has chosen to be

Archbishop of Canterbury, from that holy see? This, in our aforesaid holy father's name, Pope Innocent III, I demand of you."

King John replied, "What worldly name to interrogatories can task the free breath of a sacred King? What worldly man can force a sacred King to answer questions? You cannot, Cardinal, invent a name as slight, unworthy, and ridiculous as the name of the Pope to order me to make an answer to a question.

"Tell him what I have said, and from the mouth of the King of England add this much more, that no Italian priest — no Pope — shall tithe or toll, aka collect church revenues — in our dominions.

"As we, under Heaven, are supreme head, so under Him we will alone uphold, without the assistance of a mortal hand such as that belonging to the Pope, that great supremacy, with which we do reign.

"So tell the Pope, with all reverence to him and his usurped and stolen authority cast aside."

King Philip II said, "Brother of England, you blaspheme in doing and saying this."

King John replied, "Although you and all the Kings of Christendom are led so grossly by this meddling priest, the Pope, dreading the curse that money may buy out, and by the merit of vile gold, dross, and dust, you and the other Kings purchase the corrupted pardon of a man, who in that sale sells pardon from himself and not from God, and moreover damns himself, and although you and all the rest of the Kings so grossly led cherish this cheating witchcraft and superstition with revenue, yet I alone, alone oppose the Pope and count his friends my foes."

King John was criticizing the church's practice of selling indulgences, in which sinners paid money for the forgiveness of sins.

Cardinal Pandulph said to King John, "Then, by the lawful power that I have, you shall stand cursed and excommunicated. And blessed shall any man be who revolts from his allegiance to a heretic — you. And that hand that takes away by any secret course — such as poison — your hateful life shall be called meritorious, canonized, and worshipped as a saint."

Constance said, "Oh, let it be lawful that I can join with Rome to curse awhile! Good father Cardinal, cry amen to my keen curses, for without my wrong there is no tongue that has power to curse him right. He cannot be cursed correctly unless the wrong he has done to me is acknowledged."

"My curse is justified," Cardinal Pandulph replied. "There's law and warrant, lady, for my curse."

"And for mine, too," Constance said. "When law can do no right, then let it be lawful that law bar no wrong. Law cannot give my child his Kingdom here, for the man — King John — who holds his Kingdom upholds the law. Therefore, since law itself is perfectly wrong, how can the law forbid my tongue to curse?"

King Philip II of France and King John of England were holding hands because of the alliance that they had just arranged through marriage.

Cardinal Pandulph said, "King Philip II of France, on peril of a curse, let go of the hand of that arch-heretic, and raise up the power of France against King John's head and army, unless he submits himself to Rome."

"Why do you look pale, King of France?" Queen Eleanor asked. "Do not let go of King John's hand."

"Take action, Devil," Constance said to Queen Eleanor. "If you don't, the King of France will repent and let go of King John's hand, and Hell will lose a soul."

"King Philip II, listen to the Cardinal," the Duke of Austria advised.

"And hang a calfskin on his recreant limbs," the Bastard said.

The Duke of Austria replied, "Well, ruffian, I must pocket up and endure these wrongs, because —"

The Bastard interrupted, "— your breeches best may carry them."

King John asked, "Philip, what do you say to the Cardinal?"

"What should he say but that he agrees with the Cardinal?" Constance asked.

Louis the Dauphin said, "Think, father, about this decision. The difference is a heavy curse from Rome, or the light loss of the King of England for a friend. Forego the easier."

Blanche said, "The easier one to forego is the curse of Rome."

"Oh, Louis, stand fast!" Constance advised. "The Devil tempts you here in the likeness of a new and virgin bride."

Blanche said, "The Lady Constance speaks not from her faith, but from her need. She says not what she believes, but what she thinks will get her what she wants."

Constance said to King Philip II, "Oh, if you grant me what I need, which lives only by the death of faithfulness, that need must necessarily imply this principle: Faithfulness would live again by the death of what I need. Oh, then, trample down my need, and faithfulness mounts up. Keep my need up, and faithfulness is trodden down!"

Constance's need was for Arthur to become King of England. For that to happen, King Philip II would have to break his faithfulness — that is, he would have to break the alliance he had just faithfully sworn to King John.

King John said, "The King of France is moved — emotionally shaken — and he does not make an answer to this."

"Oh, for him to be removed from King John, and for him to answer well!" Constance said.

"Do so, King Philip," the Duke of Austria advised. "Remove yourself from King John, and hang no more in doubt."

"Hang nothing but a calfskin, most sweet lout," the Bastard said to the Duke of Austria.

"I am perplexed, and I don't know what to say," King Philip II said.

"What can you say but what will perplex you more, if you stand excommunicated and cursed?" Cardinal Pandulph said.

"Good reverend father, put yourself in my place," King Philip II said, "and tell me how you would bestow yourself. What would you do if you were me? King John's royal hand and my royal hand are newly joined, and our inward souls are conjoined and newly married in league, coupled and linked together with all the religious strength of sacred vows. The most recent breath that gave the sound of words was deeply sworn faithfulness, peace, amity, and true love between our Kingdoms and our royal selves, and just before this truce, just a little while before, no longer than we well could wash our hands to seal and settle this royal bargain of peace, Heaven knows, our hands were besmeared and stained all over with the broad paintbrush of slaughter, where revenge did paint the fearsome difference of incensed Kings.

"Shall these hands, so lately purged of blood, so newly joined in love, so strong in both, unyoke this seizure and this kind return of salutation? Play fast and loose with faith? So jest with Heaven, make such changeable and fickle children of ourselves, as now again to snatch our palm from palm, unswear and take back the faith we have sworn, and on the marriage bed of smiling peace to march a bloody army, and make a riot on the gentle brow of true sincerity?

"Oh, holy sir, my reverend father, let it not be so! Out of your grace and with the power of your office, devise, ordain, impose some gentle order and compromise and solution; and then we shall be blest to do your pleasure and continue to be friends."

"All form is formless and all order is orderless, save what is opposed and hostile to the love and friendship of the King of England," Cardinal Pandulph said. "Therefore to arms! Make war against England. Be champion of our church, or let the church, our mother, breathe her curse, a mother's curse, on her rebelling son.

"King of France, you may safer hold a serpent by the tongue, an angry lion by the deadly paw, a fasting tiger by the tooth, than keep in peace that hand which you now hold."

"I may disjoin my hand, but not my faith," King Philip II said. "I can stop holding the hand of King John, but I cannot break the faithful vow I made that I will be in alliance with him."

"And so you are making faithfulness an enemy to faith," Cardinal Pandulph said, "and like a civil war you set oath against oath, and your tongue against your tongue. Oh, let the vow you made first — the vow you made to Heaven — be the first performed to Heaven. That is, you vowed to be the champion of our church!

"The vow that you have sworn since — the vow that you swore to King John — is a vow that you have sworn against yourself and it may not be performed by yourself because that which you have sworn to do amiss is not amiss when it is truly done, and being not done, where doing tends to ill, the truth is then most done in not doing it."

Cardinal Pandulph wanted King Philip II to not keep the vow he had made to King John. The Cardinal was arguing that although it is usually unethical not to keep a vow you have sworn to keep, it is ethical not to keep an unethical vow.

Cardinal Pandulph continued, "The better act of purposes mistook is to mistake again; although deceitful, yet deceit thereby grows undeceitful, and falsehood cures falsehood, as fire cools fire within the scorched veins of one newly burned."

According to Cardinal Pandulph, it is morally right to commit a wrong if it leads one to the right path. It is morally right for King Philip II to not keep a vow if it leads to his obeying and being loyal to the church. King Philip II had committed a wrong when he made an alliance with King John. Now he needed to commit the wrong of breaking that vow because this second wrong would put him on the right path — it would make him loyal again to the church.

This society believed that exposing a burn to heat would help cure the burn. In this analogy, the burn was King Philip II's vow to be allied with England, and the heat was the breaking of that vow.

Cardinal Pandulph continued, "It is religion that makes vows be kept, but you have sworn a vow to King John that is against religion. You have sworn by your faith a vow that is against your faith. What you have sworn is against the thing you have sworn by. You have sworn an oath to God and made that oath the guarantee that you will keep that vow which goes against the will of God.

"You ought not to swear to the truth of something you are uncertain about. When you are hesitant to swear to the truth of something, you should swear only that you will not forswear and perjure yourself.

"The truth you are hesitant to swear swears only not to be forsworn. Otherwise, it would be a mockery to swear!

"You have sworn only to be not forsworn, and you will be most forsworn if you do what you have sworn to do."

King Philip II's vow contained two parts: 1) I swear by God, Whom I serve, that 2) I will form an alliance with England. King Philip II definitely wanted to keep the second part of the vow, but Cardinal Pandulph felt that King Philip II was hesitant about keeping the first part of the vow.

According to the Cardinal, the first part was the part of the vow that needed to be kept. That was the part that included the vow that the vow-maker will not be forsworn. Since that was the only part of the vow that absolutely needed to be kept, the other part of the vow — forming an alliance with England — need not be kept because it contradicted the first part.

He also meant that King Philip II had made a vow that he now needed to break, although he desperately wanted to keep that vow. King Philip II had sworn a vow to King John; that vow made him forsworn to the church. If he kept his vow to King John, he would be forsworn to the church.

Cardinal Pandulph continued, "Therefore, your later vow, which is against your first vow, is in yourself rebellion to yourself."

The vow made to King John was against the first vow that King Philip II had made, which was to support the church, and this conflict of vows led to a conflict within King Philip II. In fact, according to Cardinal Pandulph, the later vow, which conflicted with his vow to the church, made him a rebel to himself and his better nature as well as to the church.

Cardinal Pandulph continued, "And better conquest never can you make than to arm your constant and your nobler parts against these giddy loose suggestions."

The best thing for King Philip II to do, according to Cardinal Pandulph, was to reject the "giddy loose suggestions" of staying loyal to King John; instead, he should stay loyal to the church.

Cardinal Pandulph continued, "Upon which better part our prayers come in, if you allow our prayers to come in. But if you don't allow our prayers to come in, then know that the peril of our curses will light on you so heavy that you shall not shake them off, but in despair you will die under their black weight."

Religious people believe that in the case of conflicting vows, if one of the vows is made to the church and the other vow is made to an Earthly King, the vow to the church is the one that must be kept.

The Duke of Austria said, "Rebellion, flat rebellion!"

He was referring to Cardinal Pandulph's statement to King Philip II, "Therefore, your later vow against your first vow is in yourself rebellion to yourself."

"Will you never be quiet?" the Bastard said. "Wouldn't a calfskin stop that mouth of yours?"

"Father, to arms!" Louis the Dauphin advised.

"On your wedding day?" Blanche protested. "Against the blood relatives of the woman whom you have married? Shall our feast be kept with slaughtered men? Shall braying trumpets and loud churlish drums, the clamors of Hell, be the music to our wedding celebration?

"Oh, husband, listen to me! How new is the word 'husband' in my mouth! Even for that word, that name, which until this time my tongue has never pronounced, upon my knee I beg you to not go to arms against King John, my uncle."

Like Blanche, Constance now knelt and said, "Oh, upon my knee, made hard with kneeling, I pray to you, you virtuous Dauphin, don't alter the doom and judgment aforethought by Heaven!"

"Now I shall see your love," Blanche said to her husband. "What motive may be stronger with you than the name of 'wife'?"

Constance answered for Louis the Dauphin, "That which upholds him that you uphold: his honor. Oh, your honor, Louis, your honor!"

Louis the Dauphin said to his father the King, "I wonder because your majesty seems so cold and indifferent when such weighty and important considerations pull you on."

"I will proclaim a curse upon his head," Cardinal Pandulph said.

"You shall not need to," King Philip II said, making up his mind.

He said to King John, "King of England, I will fall away from you. I am your enemy now, not your ally."

Constance said, "Oh, fair return of banished majesty!"

Queen Eleanor said, "Oh, foul revolt of French inconstancy!"

King John said, "King of France, you shall rue this hour within this hour."

The Bastard said, "Old Time the clock-setter, that bald sexton Time, is it as he will? Well, then, France shall rue."

The sexton of a church both wound the clocks and dug the graves. Old Time makes a good metaphorical sexton because as time passes, all living people grow closer to the grave. With a battle fast approaching, many Frenchmen — and Englishmen — would die.

"The sun's overcast with blood," Blanche said. "Fair day, adieu! Which is the side that I must go with? I am with both sides. Each army has a hand, and in the armies' rage, I have hold of a hand of both sides. Both sides swirl asunder and dismember me.

"Louis, husband, I cannot pray that you may win.

"King John, uncle, I necessarily must pray that you may lose.

"King Philip II, father-in-law, I may not wish good fortune to be yours.

"Eleanor, grandmother, I will not wish your fortunes to thrive.

"Whoever wins, on that side I shall lose. I am assured a loss before the match is played."

Louis the Dauphin said to her, "Lady, come with me; your fortune lies with me."

"There where my fortune lives, there my life dies," Blanche replied.

"Kinsman, go draw our soldiers together," King John ordered.

The Bastard exited to carry out the order.

King John then said, "King of France, I am burned up with inflaming wrath — a rage whose heat has this condition, that nothing can allay it, nothing but blood, the blood, and the dearest-valued blood, of the King of France."

King Philip II replied, "Your rage shall burn you up, and you shall turn to ashes before our blood shall quench that fire. Look after yourself, for your life is in jeopardy."

"No more than the life of him who threatens me," King John said. "To arms! Let's hurry!"

The armies had been fighting for a while. The Bastard, holding the cut-off head of the Duke of Austria, stood on the battlefield. By killing the Duke of Austria, who had received the credit for killing Richard the Lionheart, the Bastard had avenged the death of his father. The Bastard was wearing the lion skin that had belonged to his father.

The Bastard said to himself, "Now, by my life, this day grows wondrously hot. Some airy Devil hovers in the sky and pours down mischief."

This society believed that airy demons caused such things as thunderstorms, but the Bastard was referring here to the noise of the continuing battle.

The Bastard put the head on the ground and said to himself, "The Duke of Austria's head will lie there, while I, who was once named Philip but am now named Richard, catch my breath."

King John; Arthur, who had been captured; and Hubert, who was a loyal supporter of King John, entered the scene.

King John said, "Hubert, keep this boy."

He then said to the Bastard, "Philip, move forward to the front. My mother is assailed in our tent, and I fear that she has been captured."

"My lord, I rescued her," the Bastard said. "Her highness is in a safe place, fear you not. But let's go on, my liege; for very little pain and effort will bring this labor to a happy end."

The battle was over; England had triumphed. King John, Queen Eleanor, Arthur, the Bastard, Hubert, and some lords met together.

King John said to his mother, Queen Eleanor, "So it shall be; your grace shall stay behind here in France and be very strongly guarded."

He said to Arthur, "Nephew, don't look sad. Your grandmother loves you, and your uncle will be as dear to you as your father was."

Arthur said, "Oh, this will make my mother die with grief!"

King John said to the Bastard, "Kinsman, go for England! Hasten there and arrive before us. And, before we arrive there, see that you shake the moneybags of hoarding abbots; set the imprisoned angels at liberty. The fat ribs of peace must by the hungry now be fed upon. Use our commission to its utmost force."

King John wanted the Bastard to go to England and raise money — lots of money — from the church; he wanted to empty the church's moneybags in order to pay for the war England had just fought and to feed hungry English soldiers. The "angels" were coins.

The Bastard replied, "Bell, book, and candle shall not drive me back, when gold and silver beckon me to come on. I shall not fear being excommunicated. I leave your highness."

He then said to Queen Eleanor, "Grandmother, I will pray, if I ever remember to be holy, for your fair safety, and so I kiss your hand."

"Farewell, gentle kinsman," Queen Eleanor said.

"Kinsman, farewell," King John said.

The Bastard exited.

Queen Eleanor said to Arthur, her grandson, "Come here, little grandson; listen as I talk to you."

"Come here, Hubert," King John said. "Oh, my gentle Hubert, we owe you much! Within this wall of flesh that is my body, there is a soul who accounts you her creditor and with interest means to repay your love and friendship. And my good friend, your voluntary oath of loyalty to me lives in this bosom, dearly cherished.

"Give me your hand. I had a thing to say, but I will say it at some better, more suitable time. By Heaven, Hubert, I am almost ashamed to say how well I love and respect you."

"I am much obliged to your majesty," Hubert said.

"Good friend, you have no reason to say that yet," King John said, "but you shall have reason, and even if time creeps ever so slowly, yet I shall do you good.

"I had a thing to say, but let it go. The Sun is in the Heaven, and the proud day, accompanied by the pleasures of the world, is all too gay and cheerful and too full of showy ornaments such as flowers to give me audience and listen to me.

"If the midnight bell, with its iron tongue and brazen brass mouth, sounded on into the drowsy race of night; if this same were a churchyard where we stand, and you were the owner of a thousand wrongs; or if that surly spirit, melancholy, had baked your blood and made it heavy and thick, your blood that otherwise runs tingling up and down your veins, making that idiotic jester, laughter, keep men's eyes and strain their cheeks to idle merriment, a feeling hateful to my purposes; or if that you could see me without eyes, hear me without your ears, and make a reply to me without a tongue, using your imagination alone, without eyes, ears, and the harmful sound of words; then, in despite of this brooding and watchful — like a bird watching her nestlings — day, I would pour my thoughts into your bosom.

"But, ah, I will not! Yet I love you well, and I swear that I think you love me well."

King John was hinting that he wanted Hubert to do something important for him.

"I love you so well," Hubert replied, "that whatever you tell me to do, even though my death were the inevitable result of my act, by Heaven, I swear I would do it."

"Don't I know that you would?" King John said. "Good Hubert, Hubert, Hubert, throw your eye on yonder young boy."

The young boy was Arthur, who had a claim to the throne of England.

King John continued, "I'll tell you what, my friend. He is definitely a serpent in my way, and wherever this foot of mine treads, he lies before me. Do you understand what I am saying? You are his keeper, his jailor."

"And I'll keep him in such a way," Hubert said, "that he shall not offend your majesty."

"Death," King John said bluntly.

"My lord?" Hubert said, shocked.

"A grave," King John said.

"He shall not live," Hubert said.

"Enough," King John said. "Good. I could be merry now. Hubert, I love you. Well, I'll not say what I intend to do for you. Remember."

He said to Queen Eleanor, "Madam, fare you well. I'll send those soldiers over to your majesty."

"My blessing goes with you!" Queen Eleanor replied.

"Go to England, nephew, go," King John said to young Arthur. "Hubert shall be your servant and wait on you with all true duty.

"Onward toward Calais, ho!"

Calais was a seaport.

King Philip II of France, Louis the Dauphin, and Cardinal Pandulph met together. Some attendants were present.

King Philip II said, "So, a roaring tempest on the sea has scattered a whole armada of our defeated ships and separated them from each other."

"Have courage and comfort!" Cardinal Pandulph advised. "All shall yet go well."

"What can go well, when we have run so ill?" King Philip II replied. "Are we not beaten? Is not Angiers lost? Arthur taken prisoner? Many dear friends slain? And the bloody King of England has gone into England after overpowering our resistance — he has done this in spite of me, the King of France!"

"The towns he has won, he has fortified," Louis the Dauphin said. "He has done this quickly and with good deliberation. Such temperate order in so fierce a cause is without parallel. Who has read or heard of any such action similar to this?"

"I could well endure the King of England having this praise, as long as we could find some other country that has endured the shame we endure," King Philip II said.

Constance entered the scene. She was distraught, and her hair was loose.

"Look at who is coming here!" King Philip II said. "A grave for a soul; she is holding the eternal spirit against her will, in the vile prison of afflicted breath and life. Her body is the prison of her soul."

He said to Constance, "Please, lady, come with me."

She said, "Now, now see the result of your peace."

"Patience, good lady!" King Philip II said. "Be calm! Have comfort, gentle Constance!"

"No, I defy all counsel, all redress, except that which ends all counsel, true redress," Constance said. "I mean death, death.

"Oh, amiable and lovely Death! You sweet-smelling stench! Sound and wholesome rottenness! Arise from the resting place of lasting night — Hell — you hate and terror to prosperity, and I will kiss your detestable bones and put my eyeballs in your empty eye sockets that resemble vaults. And I will ring these fingers with the worms that serve your household, and I will stop this gap of breath — my mouth — with repulsive dust and be a carrion monster like yourself."

Constance was distraught and speaking in oxymora: "You sweet-smelling stench! Sound and wholesome rottenness!"

She continued, "Come, grin at me, and I will think you smile and I will buss you as your wife. Misery's love — oh, come to me!"

Death is often portrayed as a skeleton, which has a fixed, unmoving grin rather than a smile, which involves the movement of facial muscles.

In this society, men were said to kiss their wives and buss their wantons, aka mistresses or prostitutes. "To buss" means "to sensually kiss."

"Oh, fair afflicted one, be at peace!" King Philip II said. "Be calm!"

"No, no, I will not," Constance said. "Not as long as I have breath to cry. Oh, I wish that my tongue were in the thunder's mouth! Then with an emotional outburst of grief I would shake the world, and rouse from sleep that fell anatomy — that cruel skeleton we call Death — that cannot hear a lady's feeble voice, and that scorns an ordinary incantation of a sorcerer."

"Lady, you utter madness, and not sorrow," Cardinal Pandulph said.

"You are not holy to tell such a lie about me," Constance said. "I am not mad. This hair I tear is mine. My name is Constance. I was Geoffrey's wife. Young Arthur is my son, and he is lost. I am not mad. I wish to Heaven I were mad! For if I were mad, it is likely that I would forget myself. Oh, if I could, what grief I would forget! Preach some philosophy to make me mad, and you shall be canonized, Cardinal Pandulph. Because I am not mad but am able to feel grief, my reasonable part produces a reasonable way for me to be delivered of these woes — it teaches me to kill or hang myself.

"If I were mad, I would forget my son, or madly think he were a ragdoll — a baby made of rags. I am not mad; too well, too well I feel the different plagues and afflictions of each calamity I have suffered."

"Bind up your loose tresses of hair," King Philip II said to Constance.

He then said to the others present, "Oh, what love I note in the fair multitude of her hairs! Where but by chance a silver drop — a tear — has fallen, ten thousand wiry friends — hairs — glue themselves to that drop in sociable, companionable grief, like true, inseparable, faithful loves, sticking together in calamity."

Earlier, King Philip II had requested Constance to come with him. Now she responded, "To England, if you will."

She wanted him to invade England.

"Bind up your hair," King Philip II said.

"Yes, I will do that, and why will I do it? I tore these hairs from their bonds and cried aloud, 'Oh, I wish that these hands could so redeem and free my son, just as they have given these hairs their liberty!' But now I envy their liberty, and I will again commit them to their bonds because my poor child is a prisoner."

She bound her hair.

She continued, "And, Father Cardinal Pandulph, I have heard you say that we shall see and know our friends in Heaven. If that is true, I shall see my boy again, for since the birth of Cain, the first male child, to him who just yesterday took his first breath, there was not such a creature born who was so filled with divine grace."

Cain was the first child ever born; he was also the first murderer, having murdered Abel, his brother.

Constance continued, "But now canker-sorrow and gnawing grief will eat my bud — Arthur — and chase the native beauty from his cheek and he will look as hollow as a ghost, as dim and meager as a fit of illness, and so he'll die; and, rising from death so again, when I shall meet him in the court of Heaven, I shall not know him. Therefore, never, never will I behold my pretty Arthur any more."

"You hold too terrible an opinion of grief," Cardinal Pandulph said.

"The man who talks to me never had a son," Constance said.

"You are as fond of grief as you are of your child," King Philip II said.

Constance replied, "Grief fills the room left unoccupied by my absent child, lies in his bed, walks up and down with me, puts on my son's pretty looks, repeats his words, reminds me of all his gracious qualities, stuffs his — Arthur's — vacant garments with his — grief's — form. So then, do I have reason to be fond of grief?

"Fare you well. If you had endured such a loss as I have, I could give you better comfort than you give me."

She unbound her hair again and said, "I will not keep orderly hair upon my head, when there is such disorder in my mind.

"Oh, Lord! My boy, my Arthur, my fair son! My life, my joy, my food, my all the world! My widow-comfort, and my sorrows' cure!"

She exited.

King Philip II said, "I am afraid that she may harm herself, and so I'll follow her."

He exited.

Louis the Dauphin said, "There's nothing in this world that can make me feel joy. Life is as tedious as a twice-told tale that vexes the bored ear of a drowsy man, and bitter shame has spoiled the sweet world's taste so that it yields nothing but shame and bitterness."

Cardinal Pandulph said, "Before the curing of a strong disease, even at the instant of healing and health, the fit is strongest; evils that take their leave show evil most of all on their departure. What have you lost by losing the recent battle?"

"All days of glory, joy, and happiness," Louis the Dauphin said.

"If you had won the battle, certainly you would have lost all days of glory, joy, and happiness," Cardinal Pandulph said. "When Fortune means to do the most good to men, she looks upon them with a threatening eye. It is strange to think how much King John has lost in this battle that he believes he has so clearly won. Aren't you grieved that Arthur is his prisoner?"

"As heartily as King John is glad that he has him," Louis the Dauphin replied.

Cardinal Pandulph said, "Your mind is entirely as youthful as your blood. Now listen to me speak with a prophetic spirit, for even the breath of what I mean to speak shall blow each speck of dust, each straw, each little obstacle out of the path that shall directly lead your foot to England's throne, so therefore pay close attention to what I say.

"John has seized Arthur; and it cannot be that, while warm life plays and moves in that noble youth's veins, the misplaced — wrongly placed on England's throne — John should enjoy an hour, one minute, nay, one quiet breath of rest.

"A scepter snatched with an unruly hand must be as forcefully and violently maintained as it was gained, and he who stands upon a slippery place shows no scruple about using any vile means to help him stay on top. So that John may stand, Arthur must fall. So be it, for it cannot be but so. Soon Arthur shall be dead."

"But what shall I gain by young Arthur's fall?" Louis the Dauphin asked.

"You, because of the rightful claim of Lady Blanche your wife, may then make all the claim that Arthur did," Cardinal Pandulph said. "Arthur had a rightful claim to the throne of England. Once Arthur is dead, you, because of your marriage to Blanche, will have a rightful claim to the throne of England."

"And I will lose it, life and all, as Arthur did," Louis the Dauphin replied.

"How green and inexperienced and fresh in this old world you are!" Cardinal Pandulph said. "John devises plots that you can exploit and the times conspire with you, for he who steeps his safety in true blood shall find only bloody and untrue safety. John will spill Arthur's true blood in order to secure his grasp on the throne, but that grasp will be slippery.

"This act of murder so evilly carried out shall cool the hearts of all his people and freeze their zeal, so that they will cherish and take advantage of any opportunity, no matter how small, to check his reign.

"No natural luminous appearance in the sky, no scope of nature, no distempered day, no common wind, no customary event, will occur that they do not pluck away its natural cause and call them meteors, prodigies, and signs, abnormalities, presages, and tongues of Heaven, plainly denouncing vengeance upon John."

In other words, English citizens will interpret even common, ordinary occurrences of nature as being supernatural portents calling for vengeance against King John.

Louis the Dauphin said, "Maybe John will not touch young Arthur's life, but merely keep Arthur safe and harmless as his prisoner."

Cardinal Pandulph said, "Attack England, and when John hears of your approach, if young Arthur is not already dead, then as soon as John hears the news that you have invaded England, Arthur dies. When that happens, the hearts of all John's people shall revolt from him and kiss the lips of unfamiliar change and find strong reasons for revolt and wrath in John's bloody fingertips.

"I think I see this commotion all already on foot, and even better reasons than I have named are coming into existence for you to invade England! The Bastard, who was once named Faulconbridge, is now in England, ransacking the church and offending charity. If a dozen — only a dozen! — French were there in arms, they would be as a lure to entice ten thousand English to join their side. They would be like a little snow that, tumbled about, soon becomes a mountainous avalanche.

"Oh, noble Dauphin, go with me to your father, the King. It is wonderful what may be wrought out of the Englishmen's unhappiness, now that the souls of their leaders are filled to the brim with offence and wrongdoing.

"Go to England and invade it. I will go to your father, the King of France, and urge him to do this."

"Strong reasons result in strong actions," Louis the Dauphin said. "Let us go. If you say yes, the King will not say no."

CHAPTER 4

— 4.1 —

Hubert and some executioners met in a room in the castle where Arthur was being held prisoner.

Hubert said to the executioners, "Heat these irons hot for me, and stand in the alcove behind the wall hanging. When I stamp my foot on the ground, rush forth and bind the boy whom you shall find with me fast to the chair. Be heedful. Go now, and watch."

"I hope your warrant will authorize this deed," the first executioner said.

"You have offensive scruples!" Hubert said. "Don't be afraid. Look to it — do your part."

The executioners stood behind the wall hanging.

Hubert called, "Young lad, come here; I have something to say to you."

Arthur walked into the room.

"Good morning, Hubert," Arthur said.

"Good morning, little Prince," Hubert said.

"Considering that I have so great a title to be more than a Prince — I ought to be recognized as a King! — I am as little a Prince as it is possible to be."

Looking closely at Hubert, he added, "You are sad."

"Indeed, I have been merrier," Hubert said.

"Have mercy on me!" Arthur said. "I think that nobody should be sad but I, yet I remember that when I was in France, young gentlemen like myself would be as sad as night, but only because it was a whim of theirs. By my faith as a Christian, I swear that if I were out of prison and kept sheep as a shepherd, I would be as merry as the day is long, and so I would be here, except that I am afraid that my uncle plots more harm to me. He is afraid of me, and I am afraid of him. Is it my fault that I am Geoffrey's son? No, indeed, it is not; and I wish to Heaven that I were your son, as long as you would love me, Hubert."

Hubert thought, *If I talk to him, his innocent prattling will awaken my mercy, which lies dead within me; therefore, I will be sudden and dispatch this business quickly.*

"Are you sick, Hubert?" Arthur asked. "You look pale today. Truly, I wish you were a little sick, so that I might sit up all night and stay awake with you. I assure you that I love you more than you love me."

Hubert thought, *His words take possession of my bosom. His words fill my heart.*

He said out loud, "Read this, young Arthur."

He gave Arthur a paper.

Hubert thought, *Foolish tears, what are you doing! Turning pitiless torture out of doors! I must be quick, lest my resolution drops out of my eyes in tender womanish tears.*

He said out loud, "Can't you read it? Isn't it fairly and clearly written?"

"It is written too fairly, Hubert, for so foul an effect," Arthur said. "Must you with hot irons burn out both of my eyes?"

"Young boy, I must," Hubert replied.

"And will you?" Arthur asked.

One meaning of "will" was "want," so one of the meanings of Arthur's question was "And do you want to?"

"And I will," Hubert replied.

"Have you the heart?" Arthur asked. "When your head ached, I tied my handkerchief around your brows, the best I had; a Princess embroidered it for me, and I never asked you for it again."

In this society, handkerchiefs were expensive, so Arthur was generous in not asking for it to be returned to him.

Arthur continued, "And with my hand at midnight I held your head, and like the watchful minutes to the hour, always and continually I cheered up the heavy time, saying, 'What do you need?' and 'Where does it hurt?' Or 'What good deed may I perform for you?'"

Arthur had continually talked to Hubert, making sounds, just like a clock does when it ticks.

He continued, "Many a poor man's son would have lain still and never have spoken a loving word to you, but you when you were sick had a Prince serve as your nursemaid. You may think that my love was devious love and call it cunning. Do so, if you will. If Heaven will be pleased that you must use me ill, why then you must.

"Will you put out my eyes? These eyes never did and never shall as much as frown at you."

"I have sworn to do it," Hubert said. "And with hot irons I must burn them out."

"None except those in this Iron Age would do it!" Arthur said.

People in this society believed in a historical succession of ages, aka eras, each one worse than the previous one: the Golden Age, the Silver Age, the Bronze Age, and the Iron Age. The worst was the Iron Age, which was characterized by fraud and violence.

Arthur continued, "The iron itself, although heated red-hot, as it approached near these eyes, would drink my tears and quench its fiery indignation even in the matter — the tears — of my innocence. Indeed, after that, the iron would consume itself and rust away simply because it had contained fire to harm my eyes.

"Are you more stubborn and hard than hammered iron? If an angel would have come to me and told me that Hubert would put out my eyes, I would not have believed the angel — I would believe no tongue but Hubert's."

Hubert stamped his foot on the ground and called, "Come out."

The executioners came out from their hiding place behind the wall hanging. They carried a rope, a heated iron spike, and a brazier of hot coals.

Hubert ordered, "Do what I told you to do."

Arthur pleaded, "Oh, save me, Hubert, save me! My eyes are blinded just from the fierce looks of these bloody men."

"Give me the iron, I say, and bind him here," Hubert ordered.

"Why do you need to be so violent and rough?" Arthur asked. "I will not struggle, I will stand stone-still.

"For Heaven's sake, Hubert, let me not be bound! Listen to me, Hubert, drive these men away, and I will sit as quietly as a lamb. I will not stir, nor wince, nor speak a word, nor look upon the iron angrily. Just thrust these men away, and I'll forgive you, whatever torment you inflict on me."

Hubert told the executioners, "Go and stand in another room; let me alone with him."

The first executioner said, "I am very pleased to be away from such a deed."

The executioners exited.

"I have driven away my friend!" Arthur said, referring to the first executioner. "He has a stern look, but a gentle heart. Let him come back so that his compassion may give life to yours."

"Come, boy, prepare yourself," Hubert said.

"Is there no remedy?" Arthur said. "Is there no way I can avoid being blinded?"

"None," Hubert said. "You must lose your eyes."

"Oh, Heaven, I only wish that there were a mote in your eyes, a grain, a dust, a gnat, a wandering hair, any annoyance in that precious sense of eyesight!" Arthur said. "Then feeling what small things are irritable and painful there, your vile intent to put a hot iron in my eyes must necessarily seem horrible to you."

"Are you doing what you promised to do once I sent away the executioners?" Hubert asked. "You promised to be quiet. Hold your tongue."

"Hubert, a pair of tongues is unable to plead adequately for a pair of eyes," Arthur said. "Let me not hold my tongue, let me not, Hubert. Or, Hubert, if you will, cut out my tongue and let me keep my eyes. Oh, spare my eyes even if their only use is always to look at you!

"Look, I swear that the instrument of blinding is cold and would not harm me."

"I can heat it, boy," Hubert said.

"No, truly the fire is dead with grief," Arthur said. "Being created for comfort, it died rather than be used to inflict undeserved acts of cruelty.

"See for yourself. There is no malice in this burning coal; the breath of Heaven has blown its spirit out and strewn repentant ashes on its head."

"But with my breath I can revive it, boy," Hubert said. "I can blow on it and make it glow."

"If you do, you will only make it blush and glow with shame at your proceedings, Hubert," Arthur said. "Perhaps it will throw sparks in your eyes, and like a dog that is compelled to fight, it will snatch at its master who incites him to fight.

"All things that you should use to do me wrong deny their service to you. Only you lack that mercy which fierce fire and iron extends to me; fire and iron are noted for their merciless uses."

"Well, see to live," Hubert said. "You will be able to see so that you can take care of your living self. I will not touch your eyes for all the treasure that your uncle — King John — owns. Yet I swore and I did intend, boy, with this same iron to burn out your eyes."

"Oh, now you look like Hubert!" Arthur said. "You were disguised all this time."

"Peace; say no more," Hubert said. "Adieu. Your uncle must not hear anything except that you are dead. I'll fill these fierce, cruel spies with false reports of your death. Pretty child, you shall sleep safe and without fear and secure, knowing that Hubert, for the wealth of all the world, will not hurt you."

"Oh, Heaven!" Arthur said. "I thank you, Hubert."

"Silence; say no more," Hubert said. "Stay close to me and secretly go in with me. I am undergoing much danger for you."

King John, the Earl of Pembroke, the Earl of Salisbury, and some other lords met. King John had recently been crowned again. When he had been excommunicated, his subjects had been released from their vows of loyalty to him. When King John was crowned again, his subjects renewed their vows of loyalty. The other lords did not think that it had been necessary for King John to be crowned again.

Using the royal plural, King John said, "Here once again we sit, once again crowned, and looked upon, I hope, with cheerful eyes."

"This 'once again,' except that it pleased your highness, was superfluous," the Earl of Pembroke said. "You have been crowned one time too many. You were crowned before, and that high royalty — your crown — was never plucked from off your head, and the faiths of your subjects were never stained and spoiled with revolt. Your subjects never troubled the land with fresh anticipation of any longed-for change or better government."

The Earl of Salisbury said, "Therefore, to be possessed with double pomp, to adorn a title that was rich before, to gild refined gold, to paint a lily, to throw perfume on the violet, to smooth ice, or add another hue to the rainbow, or light a candle in hopes of adding beauty to the Sun — the beauteous eye of Heaven — is wasteful and ridiculous excess."

"Except that your royal pleasure must be done," the Earl of Pembroke said, "this act is like an ancient tale told again, and in the last repeating troublesome, being urged at a time unseasonable. It is like repeating a story that is already well-known and does not need repeating — and in addition telling it at a bad and inconvenient time."

The Earl of Salisbury said, "In this the ancient and well-known face of plain old form — simple customary behavior — is much disfigured, and, like a change of wind blowing into a sail, it makes the course of thoughts fetch about and change direction, it startles and frightens thought, and it makes sound opinion sick and truth be suspected, because you have put on so new a fashioned robe."

His point was that by having a second, unnecessary coronation, King John was causing people to wonder why it had been held. Did King John feel it was needed because of a weak claim on the throne?

The reference to "so new a fashioned robe" meant 1) a new coronation robe as opposed to the one King John had worn when he was first crowned, and 2) a robe of a new style, rather than the robe of "plain old form," aka a coronation done in the customary manner.

The Earl of Pembroke said, "When workmen strive to do better than well, they confound their skill and harm their work because of greediness to do even better. Often the excusing of a fault makes the fault worse because of the excuse. It is like patches set upon a little tear that discredit more in the hiding of the fault than did the fault before it was so patched. A small tear may not be noticed; a large patch will definitely be noticed."

"We made these points when we gave advice to you before you were newly crowned," the Earl of Salisbury said, "but it pleased your highness to overrule our advice, and we are all well pleased, since all and every part of what we would, aka wish, makes a stand at what your highness will."

"Makes a stand" is ambiguous. The phrase can mean "halt," in which case the Earl of Salisbury was saying that he and the other lords would halt their own wishes when King John overruled them. The phrase can also mean "stand up to," in which case the Earl of Salisbury was saying that he and the other lords would stand up to King John.

Although the Earl of Salisbury had said that he and the other lords were "all well pleased," in fact they were not.

King John said, "Some reasons for this second coronation I have informed you of, and I think that the reasons are strong. Later, when lesser is my fear, I shall give you more reasons that are stronger than these."

He may have been referring to a time after Arthur was dead; Arthur's death would lessen his fear of losing his crown.

He continued, "In the meantime, ask about what you would have reformed that is not already well, and well shall you perceive how willingly I will both hear you and grant you your requests. Make a petition to me now."

The Earl of Pembroke said, "Then I, as the one who is the spokesman of these lords present in order to express the proposals of all their hearts, both for myself and them, but chief of all for your safety and security, for the which

I myself and they direct our best efforts, heartily request the enfranchisement of Arthur. We want him to be released from prison because his imprisonment moves the murmuring lips of discontent to break into this dangerous argument: If you rightfully hold what in peacetime you have, why should then your fears, which, as they say, attend the steps of wrong, move you to coop up your tender kinsman and to choke his days with barbarous ignorance and deny his youth the rich advantage of good exercise, training, and education? If you are rightfully King, why should Arthur be imprisoned?

"So that the time's enemies — those opposed to the current state of affairs — may not have this to use as an excuse for discontent, let our petition that you have bid us to ask be for his liberty, which for our goods we no further ask than to the extent that our welfare, which depends on you, counts it as your welfare that he have his liberty."

The Earl of Pembroke and the other lords wanted Arthur to be set free because they believed that this would be in King John's best interest.

Hubert entered the room.

"Let it be done," King John said. "Arthur shall be set free, and I commit his youth to your direction. You shall supervise his education.

"Hubert, what news did you bring with you?"

He and Hubert talked quietly; the others could not hear them.

The Earl of Pembroke said quietly to the other lords so that King John and Hubert could not hear him, "This — Hubert — is the man who would do the bloody deed of killing Arthur. He showed his warrant to a friend of mine. The image of a wicked heinous sin and crime lives in his eye; that secretive appearance of his shows the mood of a much-troubled breast, and I fearfully believe that he has done that which we so feared he had orders to do."

The Earl of Salisbury said, "The color of the King's face comes and goes between his purpose and his conscience. The color changes from red to white depending on whether he is happy he has achieved his aim or is horrified at the evil he has done. The color is like red-wearing heralds going between two dreadful armies set up for battle: The red comes and goes. His passion is so ripe that it necessarily must break. His emotion is so strong that it will break out like the bursting of a boil."

The Earl of Pembroke said, "And when it breaks, I fear that the foul corruption of a sweet child's death will issue from it."

King John said, "We cannot hold mortality's strong hand."

This meant 1) Even I, the King, cannot keep death away from the living, and 2) Even I, the King, cannot survive grasping mortality's strong hand; I, the King, will also die. In other words, all of us are mortal.

He continued, "Good lords, although my will to give is living, the request that you demand is gone and dead. Hubert tells us that Arthur died last night."

"Indeed, we feared his sickness was past cure," the Earl of Salisbury said.

"Indeed, we heard how near his death he was before the child himself felt he was sick," the Earl of Pembroke said.

In other words, the lords believed that Arthur had not died of illness but had been murdered.

The Earl of Pembroke continued, "This must be answered and accounted for either here or hence."

"Hence" meant in the afterlife.

"Why do you bend such solemn brows on me?" King John asked. "Why do you frown at me? Do you think I bear the shears of destiny? Do I command the pulse of life?"

The three Fates commanded the pulse of life; they controlled human life. Clotho spun the thread of life. Lachesis measured the thread of life, determining how long a person lived. Atropos cut the thread of life; when the thread was cut, the person died.

"This is obvious foul play," the Earl of Salisbury said, "and it is shameful that greatness — a King — should so blatantly inflict it. May your game — your intrigue — end with the same result! And so, farewell."

The Earl of Pembroke said, "Wait a moment, Lord Salisbury. I'll go with you, and find the inheritance of this poor child — his little Kingdom of a grave that he violently inherited. That blood — that life — which owned the breadth of this isle, now holds and owns just three feet of it. It's a bad world when such things happen! This evil must not be thus endured. This evil will break out to all our sorrows, and before long I fear."

The lords exited.

"They burn in indignation," King John said. "I repent because my plan did not work. There is no sure foundation set on blood, no certain life achieved by others' death."

A messenger entered the room.

King John said to him, "You have a fearful and frightening eye. Where is the blood that I have seen inhabit those cheeks of yours? So foul a sky does not clear without a storm. Pour down your weather and news, which must be bad. How goes all in France?"

"All in France move from France to England," the messenger said. "Never has such an army for any foreign invasion been before levied in the body of a land. They have learned from your example of doing things speedily. At the time you should be told that they are preparing to invade England, the news instead comes that they have all arrived and invaded England."

"Oh, where has our intelligence — the people who should have gathered this information — been drunk?" King John said. "Where has it slept? Where is my mother's care? How can such an army be gathered in France, and she not hear of it?"

"My liege, your mother's ear is stopped with dust," the messenger said. "Your noble mother died on the first of April, and I hear, my lord, that the Lady Constance died in a delirious frenzy three days before your mother died, but this information comes from a rumor I idly heard without paying much attention to it. I don't know whether it is true or false."

"Withhold your speed, dreadful events!" King John said. "Oh, make a treaty with me until I have pleased my discontented peers! Bad news is coming to me too quickly.

"My mother is dead! How wildly then walks my estate in France! My affairs in France that my mother was taking care of are now disordered!

"Under whose leadership came those armies of France that you tell me have truly landed here?"

"They are under the leadership of Louis the Dauphin," the messenger said.

"You have bewildered me with these ill tidings," King John said.

The Bastard entered the room. With him was Peter of Pomfret.

King John said, "Now, what says the world to your proceedings? What is the reaction to what you have done under my orders? Do not seek to stuff my head with more ill news, for it is full."

"If you are afraid to hear the worst," the Bastard said, "then let the worst unheard fall on your head."

Two proverbs of the time were 1) "It is good to fear the worst" and 2) "To know the worst is good." If you know and fear the worst, you can take steps to deal with it.

"Bear with me, kinsman," King John said, "because I was bewildered under the tide of bad news, but now I breathe again aloft the flood of bad news, and can pay attention to any tongue, whatever news it brings."

"How I have fared among the clergymen, the sums I have collected shall express," the Bastard said. "But as I labored and traveled here through the land, I found the people full of strange fantasies. They are possessed by rumors, full of idle dreams, not knowing what they fear, but full of fear.

"And this man here is a prophet, whom I brought with me from the streets of Pomfret. I found him with many hundreds treading on his heels; to them he sang, in rude harsh-sounding rhymes, that, before the next Ascension Day at noon, your highness should deliver up your crown."

Ascension Day commemorates the ascension of Jesus Christ — bodily — into Heaven.

King John said to Peter of Pomfret, "You idle dreamer, why did you do that?"

"Because I have foreknowledge," Peter of Pomfret said. "I know that this will truly happen."

"Hubert, take this man away," King John said. "Imprison him, and at noon on that day which he says I shall yield up my crown, let him be hanged. Take him to a prison, and then return, for I must make use of you."

Hubert exited with Peter of Pomfret.

King John said to the Bastard, "Oh, my gentle cousin, have you heard the news that is abroad about who have arrived on our shores?"

"The French, my lord," the Bastard replied. "Men's mouths are full of the news. Besides, I met Lord Bigot and Lord Salisbury, who have eyes as red as newly kindled fire, and others as well, who were going to seek the grave of Arthur, who they say was killed last night at your instigation."

"Gentle kinsman, go, and thrust yourself into their companies," King John said. "Join them. I have a way to win their loves again; bring them before me."

King John may have been willing to execute Hubert in order to appease the nobles.

"I will seek them out," the Bastard said.

"Make haste," King John said. "Put the better foot before you and go as fast as you can! Oh, let me have no enemies who are my subjects, not when adverse foreigners frighten my towns and cause dread with their show of determined invasion! Be Mercury, attach feathers to your heels, and fly as fast as thought from them to me again."

Mercury, the messenger of the gods, wore winged sandals. In some myths, he had winged feet.

"The spirit of the time shall teach me speed," the Bastard said. "Speed is necessary at this time."

He exited.

King John said, "Spoken like a spirited noble gentleman."

He then said to the messenger, "Go after him, for he perhaps shall need some messenger to go between me and the peers; you shall be that messenger."

"With all my heart, my liege," the messenger said.

He exited.

"My mother is dead!" King John said.

Hubert entered the room.

"My lord, they say five moons were seen last night," Hubert said. "Four were fixed and did not move, and the fifth whirled about the other four in a bizarre motion."

"Five moons!" King John said.

"Old men and beldams — crones — in the streets prophesy upon the sight ominously and daringly. Young Arthur's death is common gossip in their mouths, and when they talk about him, they shake their heads and whisper to one another in the ear, and he who speaks grips the hearer's wrist, while he who hears reacts in fear, with wrinkled brows, with nods, and with rolling eyes.

"I saw a blacksmith stand with his hammer, like this" — he demonstrated — "while his iron cooled on the anvil, with open mouth swallowing a tailor's news. The tailor, with his shears and measuring tape in his hand, standing in slippers, which in his nimble haste he had incorrectly thrust upon the wrong feet, told of many thousand warlike French who were marshaled for fight and drawn up in battle positions in Kent.

"Another lean unwashed artificer cut off the tailor's tale and talked about Arthur's death."

"Why do you seek to possess me with these fears?" King John asked. "Why did you urge me so often to cause young Arthur's death? Your hand has murdered him. I had a mighty reason to wish him dead, but you had none to kill him."

"Had no reason, my lord?" Hubert said. "Why, didn't you incite me to kill him?"

King John said, "It is the curse of Kings to be served by slaves who take their whims for a warrant to break within the blood-containing house of life, and when the King shuts his eyes such slaves infer a law and suppose themselves to know the meaning of dangerous majesty, when perhaps majesty frowns more because of a whim than because of a deliberate and carefully considered decision."

Showing King John a document, Hubert replied, "Here is your signature and seal authorizing what I did."

King John replied, "Oh, when the last account between Heaven and Earth is to be made and we are judged, then this signature and seal shall be witnesses against us and damn us!

"How often the sight of means to do ill deeds makes deeds ill done! If you had not been nearby — you, who are a fellow by the hand of nature noted, written down, and confirmed with a signature to do a deed of shame — this murder had not come into my mind. But taking note of your abhorred appearance, and finding you fit for bloody villainy and apt and liable to be employed in danger, I half-heartedly mentioned Arthur's death to you, and you, to be endeared to a King, made it no matter of conscience to destroy a Prince."

"My lord —" Hubert began.

King John interrupted, "Had you only shook your head or paused when I spoke darkly and obscurely what I purposed, or turned an eye of doubt upon my face, as if you were asking me to tell my tale in explicit words, deep shame would have struck me dumb and made me break off, and those fears of yours might have wrought fears in me. But you understood me by my signs and did in signs again parley with sin.

"Yes, without a pause you let your heart consent, and consequently your rude hand enacted the deed, which both of our tongues held vile to name.

"Get out of my sight, and never see me anymore! My nobles leave me, and my government is challenged, even at my gates, with ranks of foreign troops.

"Indeed, in the body of this fleshly land of mine, this Kingdom, this confine of blood and breath, hostility and civil tumult reign between my conscience and my nephew's death."

"Arm yourself against your other enemies," Hubert said. "I'll make a peace between your soul and you. Young Arthur is alive. This hand of mine is still a maiden and an innocent hand; it is not painted with the crimson spots of blood. Within this bosom never entered yet the dreadful emotion of a murderous thought, and you have slandered nature in my form, which, however rude exteriorly, is yet the cover of a fairer mind than to be butcher of an innocent child."

"Does Arthur live?" King John said. "Oh, hasten to the peers, throw this report on their incensed rage, and make them tame to their obedience! When the lords hear that Arthur lives, they will again obey me.

"Forgive the comment that I in my anger made about your appearance, for my rage was blind, and foul imaginary eyes of blood presented yourself as more hideous than you are.

"Don't answer me, for there is no time, but to my private chamber bring the angry lords with all expedient haste.

"I beseech you only slowly; run faster than I beseech you."

Arthur, wearing the clothing of a ship-boy, stood on a wall of the castle in which he was imprisoned.

He said to himself, "The wall is high, and yet I will leap down. Good ground, be pitiful and don't hurt me! There's few or none who know me. If they see me, this ship-boy's appearance has quite disguised me. I am afraid to jump, and yet I'll venture it. If I get down, and do not break my limbs, I'll find a thousand stratagems to get away. It's as good to die and go, as to die and stay. It's as good to die while attempting an escape as to stay and die at my uncle's orders."

He jumped — and fell hard on the rocks below.

He said, "Oh, me! My uncle's hard spirit is in these hard stones. I am mortally hurt. May Heaven take my soul, and may England keep my bones!"

He died.

The Earl of Pembroke, the Earl of Salisbury, and Lord Bigot arrived on the scene.

Talking about Louis the Dauphin, the Earl of Salisbury said, "Lords, I will meet him at Saint Edmundsbury. It is our best safeguard, and we must welcome this courteous offer at this perilous time."

"Who brought that letter from the Cardinal?" the Earl of Pembroke asked.

The Earl of Salisbury replied, "The Count Melun, a noble lord of France, whose private communication to me of the Dauphin's friendship is much more comprehensive than these lines import."

Lord Bigot said, "Tomorrow morning let us meet him then."

"Or rather let us then set forward," the Earl of Salisbury said, "for it will be two long days' journey, lords, before we meet him."

The Bastard entered the scene.

"Once more today well met, distempered lords!" he greeted them.

Earlier that day, the Bastard had met them as they set out to find Arthur's grave.

The Bastard continued, "The King by me requests your presence immediately."

"The King has dispossessed himself of us," the Earl of Salisbury said. "We will not line his thin and stained cloak with our pure honors, nor serve the foot that leaves the print of blood wherever it walks. We will not serve and obey him. Return and tell him that. We know the worst. We know that he had Arthur killed."

"I will say whatever you think, but good words, I think, would be best to send to the King," the Bastard said.

"Our griefs, and not our manners, reason now," the Earl of Salisbury said. "Our grievances talk for us; we no longer observe courtesy when it comes to the King."

"But there is little reason in your grief," the Bastard said. "Therefore, it would be reasonable if you had manners now."

"Sir, sir, anger has its privilege," the Earl of Pembroke said.

"That is true," the Bastard said. "Anger has the privilege to hurt the one who is angry; it does not have the privilege to hurt anyone else."

A proverb of the time stated, "Anger punishes itself."

They had been traveling as they talked, and the Earl of Salisbury said, "This is the prison."

Seeing the corpse of Arthur, the Earl of Salisbury asked, "Who is he who is lying here?"

Recognizing Arthur, the Earl of Pembroke said, "Oh, death, made proud with pure and Princely beauty! The earth had not a hole to hide this deed. No grave could hide this murder."

The Earl of Salisbury said, "Murder, hating what itself has done, lays this murder out in the open to urge on revenge."

Lord Bigot said, "Or, when he doomed this beauty to a grave, found it too precious-Princely for a grave."

The corpses of Kings and Princes were not buried in graves; they were embalmed and placed in mausoleums and tombs.

"Sir Richard, what do you think?" the Earl of Salisbury asked. "Have you beheld, or have you read or heard anything like this? Could you think that such a thing could happen? Do you almost doubt, although you see it, that you see it? Could thought, without this object, form such another? This is the very top, the height, the crest, or the crest upon the crest, of murder's aims. This is the bloodiest shame, the wildest savagery, the vilest stroke, that ever glaring-eyed wrath or staring rage presented to the tears of soft remorse."

"All past murders are excused because of this inexcusable murder," the Earl of Pembroke said. "And this murder, so sole and so unmatchable, shall give a holiness, a purity, to the yet unbegotten sins of times to come and show that a deadly bloodshed is only a jest in comparison to this heinous spectacle."

"It is a damned and a bloody work," the Bastard said. "It was done by the graceless action of a heavy hand, if this is the work of any hand."

"If it is the work of any hand!" the Earl of Salisbury said. "We had a kind of inkling of what would ensue. This murder is the shameful work of Hubert's hand, and the stratagem and the plan of the King, whom I forbid my soul ever to obey."

He knelt and said, "Kneeling before this ruin of sweet life, and breathing to Arthur's breathless excellence the incense of a vow, a holy vow, I vow never to taste the pleasures of the world, never to be infected with delight — to enjoy delight while such a murder is unavenged is an illness — nor be conversant with ease and idleness, until I have made this hand glorious by giving it the honor of revenge."

"Our souls religiously confirm your words," the Earl of Pembroke and Lord Bigot said.

The Earl of Salisbury stood up.

Hubert arrived.

Not seeing the corpse of Arthur, he said, "Lords, I am hot with haste in seeking you. Arthur is still alive; the King has sent for you."

The Earl of Salisbury said, "Oh, he is old and does not blush at death. Avaunt — leave! — you hateful villain. Get thee gone!"

The word "thee" was less formal and less respectful than the word "you."

"I am no villain," Hubert said.

"Must I rob the law?" the Earl of Salisbury said, drawing his sword.

By killing Hubert before Hubert had a fair trial, the Earl of Salisbury would be robbing the law, which would, he thought, sentence Hubert to death.

"Your sword is bright, sir; put it up again," the Bastard said. "Sheath your sword."

A bright sword is unused; the Bastard's implication was that the Earl of Salisbury's sword was for decorative purposes only.

"Not until I sheathe it in a murderer's skin," the Earl of Salisbury said.

"Stand back, Lord Salisbury, stand back, I say," Hubert said. "By Heaven, I think my sword's as sharp as yours. I would not have you, lord, forget yourself, nor tempt the danger of my true defense, lest I, by paying attention only to your rage, forget your worth, your greatness, and your nobility."

"Get out, dunghill!" Lord Bigot said. "Do you dare to challenge a nobleman?"

Hubert's social class was lower than that of the lords.

"Not for my life," Hubert said, "but yet I dare to defend my innocent life against an Emperor."

The Earl of Salisbury said, "You are a murderer."

"Do not prove that I am a murderer by making me kill you," Hubert said. "As of now, I am no murderer. Whoever speaks falsely, speaks not truly; whoever speaks not truly, lies."

In this society, these were close to fighting words. Hubert was close to calling the Earl of Salisbury a liar. Two noblemen would fight a duel if one called the other a liar. If a commoner called a nobleman a liar, the nobleman would probably attack him. In this culture, however, a high-ranking man would often refrain from killing a low-ranking man, regarding such a deed as beneath him.

"Cut him to pieces," the Earl of Pembroke said.

"Keep the peace, I say," the Bastard said.

"Stand aside, or I shall wound you, Faulconbridge," the Earl of Salisbury said to the Bastard.

"You would be better off if you wounded the Devil, Salisbury," the Bastard said. "If you only frown at me, or move your foot, or direct your hasty anger to do me shame, I'll strike you dead. Put up your sword immediately; or I'll so maul you and your toasting-iron — your sword, which you use only for toasting cheese — that you shall think the Devil has come from Hell."

"Is this what you want to do, renowned Faulconbridge?" Lord Bigot said. "Second — that is, support — a villain and a murderer?"

Hubert said, "Lord Bigot, I am neither a villain nor a murderer."

"Who killed this Prince?" Lord Bigot said, pointing to Arthur's corpse.

Seeing the corpse for the first time, and recognizing Arthur, Hubert said, "An hour has not passed since I left him alive and well. I honored him, I loved him, and I will weep the rest of my life for the loss of his sweet life."

He wept.

The Earl of Salisbury said, "Trust not those cunning waters of his eyes, for villainy is not without such tears, and he, long experienced in villainy, makes his eyes' water seem like rivers of remorse and innocence. Come away with me, all you whose souls abhor the unclean, morally impure stinks of a slaughterhouse, for I am choked by this smell of sin."

Lord Bigot said, "Let's go toward Saint Edmundsbury to see Louis the Dauphin there!"

The Earl of Pembroke said to the Bastard, "Tell the King he may find us there."

The lords exited.

"Here's a good world!" the Bastard said sarcastically. "Here's a mess!"

He asked Hubert, "Did you know about this 'fair' work? If you did this deed of death, then you are beyond the infinite and boundless reach of mercy, and you are damned, Hubert."

"Listen to me, sir," Hubert said.

"Ha!" the Bastard said. "I'll tell you what. You are damned as black — no, nothing is as black and damned as you are black and damned — you are more deeply damned than Prince Lucifer. There is not yet so ugly a fiend of Hell as you shall be, if you killed this child."

"Upon my soul —" Hubert began.

The Bastard interrupted, "If you even just consented to this most cruel act, do nothing but despair because you are already damned. And if you need a cord, the smallest thread that a spider ever twisted from her womb will be enough to strangle you, a slender reed will be a beam you can use to hang yourself on, or if you want to drown yourself, put just a little water in a spoon, and it shall be like all the ocean, enough to drown such a villain as you. I suspect you very seriously."

Many people of the time believed, "The greater the villain, the worse the fortune."

Hubert replied, "If I in act, consent, or sin of thought am guilty of stealing that sweet breath which was enclosed in this beauteous clay — Arthur's body

— then let Hell lack enough pains to torture me. Let Hell torture me with every torment it has. When I left Arthur, he was well."

"Go, carry him in your arms," the Bastard said. "I am amazed and bewildered, I think, and I lose my way among the maze of thorns and dangers of this world."

Hubert picked up Arthur's body.

The Bastard said, "How easily you take all England up!"

"All England" literally meant "the rightful King of England." Figuratively, it referred to the country of England. Arthur's death would have bad effects on England. Already it had caused some English lords to desert King John and go over to the side of Louis the Dauphin.

The Bastard continued, "From forth this morsel of dead royalty, the life and the right and the truth of all this realm has fled to Heaven, and England now is left to tug and scramble and to tear by the teeth the disputed ownership of the proud-swelling state — it is disputed because the rightful English King is dead.

"Now for the bare-picked bone of majesty, dogged war bristles his angry crest and snarls in the gentle eyes of peace. Now French armies away from their home and discontents here at home in England meet in one line and fight on the same side, and vast confusion waits — as a raven waits for a sick, fallen beast to die — for the imminent decay and destruction of usurped Kingship.

"Now happy is he whose cloak and belt can withstand this tempest."

He said to Hubert, "Carry away that child and follow me with speed. I'll go to King John. A thousand pressing matters are at hand, and Heaven itself frowns upon the land."

CHAPTER 5

— 5.1 —

King John, Cardinal Pandulph, and some attendants were in a room of the King's palace. Cardinal Pandulph was holding King John's crown.

King John said to Cardinal Pandulph, "Thus have I yielded into your hand the circle — the crown — of my glory."

Cardinal Pandulph gave the crown to King John and said, "Take again from this my hand — as a grant from the Pope — your sovereign greatness and authority."

King John put the crown on his head and said, "Now keep your holy word. Go and meet the French, and use all your power from his Holiness to stop their marches before we are engulfed with fire.

"Our discontented counties — shires and lords — revolt; our people refuse to practice obedience, instead swearing allegiance and the love of their soul to foreign blood, to foreign royalty.

"This inundation of diseased dispositions can be made healthy again only by you. So don't pause, for the present time is so sick that medicine must be immediately ministered, or else an incurable destruction will ensue."

Cardinal Pandulph replied, "It was my breath that blew this tempest up, following your stubborn treatment of the Pope, but since you are a gentle convert and are again obedient to the church, my tongue shall hush again this storm of war and make fair weather in your blustering land.

"On this Ascension Day, remember well that I, following upon your oath of service to the Pope, go and make the French lay down their arms."

He exited.

King John said, "Is this Ascension Day? Didn't the prophet say that before Ascension Day at noon I should give up my crown? And so I have. I thought that I should give it up on constraint and force, but Heaven be thanked, I gave it up only voluntarily."

The Bastard entered the room and delivered this bad news: "All Kent has yielded; nothing there holds out except Dover Castle. London has received, like a kind host of an inn, the Dauphin and his armies. Your nobles will not listen to you, but have gone to offer their service to your enemy, and wild amazement and bewilderment hurry up and down the small number of your worried, fearful friends — friends whose loyalty to you can be doubted."

"Wouldn't my lords return to me and be loyal again, after they heard that young Arthur was alive?" King John asked.

"They found him dead and cast into the streets," the Bastard said. "He was an empty casket, where the jewel of life by some damned hand was robbed and taken away."

"That villain Hubert told me that young Arthur lived," King John said.

"So, on my soul, Arthur did live, for anything Hubert knew," the Bastard said. "Hubert sincerely thought that Arthur was alive. But why do you droop? Why do you look sad? Be great in act, as you have been in thought. Don't let the world see fear and serious doubt govern the motion of a Kingly eye. Be as stirring as the time; be fire with fire; threaten the threatener and defy and intimidate the brow of threatening horror. If you do this, inferior eyes, which borrow their behaviors from the great, will grow great by your example and put on the dauntless spirit of resolution.

"Go, and glisten like Mars, the god of war, when he intends to grace and honor the battlefield. Show boldness and aspiring confidence.

"What, shall they seek the lion in his den — the King in his country — and frighten him and make him tremble there? Oh, let it not be said. Range abroad and seek the enemy, and run to meet displeasure farther from the doors, and grapple with him before he comes so near."

King John said, "The legate of the Pope has been with me, and I have made a happy peace with him: He has promised to dismiss the armies led by the Dauphin."

"Oh, what an inglorious, shameful, and humiliating league and alliance!" the Bastard said. "Shall we, upon the footing of our own land, send fair-play orders and make compromise, insinuation, parley, and base truce to an invading army?

"Shall a beardless boy — the Dauphin, who is a pampered, spoiled child — confront our battlefields, and flesh his spirit in a warlike soil, mocking the air with colors idly spread, and find no check?"

"To flesh a sword" meant "to cover it with an enemy's blood." Here the Bastard was complaining that a representative of the Pope would make peace when the Bastard preferred to fight.

The Bastard continued, "Let us, my liege, go to arms. Let's prepare to fight. Perhaps Cardinal Pandulph cannot make your peace, or if he does, let it at least be said that the French saw that we intended to defend ourselves against their invasion."

"You have the management of this present time," King John said. "Do what you said you want to do. Prepare an army."

"Let's leave, then, with good courage!" the Bastard said. "Yet, I know, our party may well meet a prouder foe."

His last words were ambiguous and could mean 1) Our army could very well meet a prouder and more courageous army than our army is, or 2) Our army could very well fight off a prouder and more courageous army than the one the Dauphin has brought.

Louis the Dauphin, the Earl of Salisbury, Lord Melun, the Earl of Pembroke, and Lord Bigot met in Louis the Dauphin's camp at Saint Edmundsbury. Some French soldiers were present.

Louis the Dauphin handed Lord Melun a document and said, "My Lord Melun, let this be copied out, and keep it safe for our memory. Return the original to these English lords again, so that, having our fair and equitable agreement written down, both they and we, perusing over these notes, may know why we took the sacrament and keep our faiths firm and inviolable."

In this culture, people would take communion in order to sanctify a treaty or agreement.

The Earl of Salisbury said, "Upon our sides our agreement never shall be broken. Noble Dauphin, although we swear a voluntary zeal and an uncompelled faith to your proceedings, yet believe me, Prince, I am not glad that such a sore of the present time should seek a healing bandage by despised revolution and heal the inveterate corruption of one wound — Arthur's death — by making many. The present time is ill and must be healed — unfortunately — by rebellion against King John.

"It grieves my soul that I must draw this metal sword from my side to be a widow-maker there where honorable rescue and defense cries out upon the name of Salisbury!"

The Earl of Salisbury was conflicted. He believed that he was honorably rescuing England by rebelling against King John and so honorable rescue cried out in support of the name of Salisbury, but he was also supporting a French army's invasion of England and so honorable defense cried out against the name of Salisbury.

He continued, "But such is the infection of the time that, for the health and medicine of our right, we cannot act except with the very hand of stern injustice and confused wrong. And isn't it a pity, my grieved and unhappy friends, that we, the sons and children of this isle, were born to see so sad an hour as this, wherein we step after a foreigner, march upon her gentle bosom, and fill up our country's enemies' ranks? I must withdraw and weep upon the stain of this cause forced upon us — to favor the gentry of a remote land and follow unfamiliar battle flags here.

"What, here? Oh, my nation, I wish that you could move yourself away from here! I wish that Neptune's arms, which hug you, could bear you away from the knowledge of yourself, and grapple you to a pagan shore, where these two Christian armies might join the blood of malice in a vein of league, and not spend it so unneighborly!"

Neptune is the Roman god of the ocean. By saying that Neptune's arms hug England, the Earl of Salisbury meant that it was an island country.

"You show a noble temperament in this emotion of yours," Louis the Dauphin said. "Great emotions wrestling in your bosom make an earthquake of nobility."

In this culture, people believed that violent winds under the surface of the earth caused earthquakes.

He continued, "Oh, what a noble combat you have fought between compulsion and a worthy, excellent respect — between what you have been forced to do and the brave consideration of your true duty!"

Wiping away the tears from the Earl of Salisbury's face, Louis the Dauphin said, "Let me wipe off this honorable dew that with a silvery appearance trickles down your cheeks. My heart has melted at a lady's tears, which are an ordinary inundation, but this effusion of such manly drops, this shower, blown up by a tempest in the soul, startles my eyes, and makes me more amazed than if I had seen the domed top of Heaven decorated all over with burning meteors.

"Lift up your brow, renowned Salisbury, and with a great heart heave and thrust away the storm. Hand over these waters to those eyes of a baby who never saw the giant adult world enraged, nor met with fortune other than at feasts, completely full of warm emotions, of mirth, and of merrymaking.

"Come, come; for you shall thrust your hand as deep into the purse of rich prosperity as I — Louis myself — do. And so, nobles, shall you all, all you who knit your sinews to the strength of my sinews.

"And even there, I think, an angel spoke."

One kind of angel was a coin. Louis the Dauphin had promised to pay the English lords for their support. Here he may have been contemptuous of the English lords, although he would have been careful not to show it.

Cardinal Pandulph arrived.

Seeing him, Louis the Dauphin said, "Look where the holy legate is coming in order to give us authorization from the hand of Heaven and on our actions to set like a seal on a warrant the name of right with holy breath."

"Hail, noble Prince of France!" Cardinal Pandulph said to Louis the Dauphin. "The news is this: King John has reconciled himself with Rome; his spirit has submitted that so stood out against the holy church, the great metropolis and jurisdiction of Rome.

"Therefore, now wind up your threatening battle flags, and tame the savage spirit of wild war, so that like a lion reared by hand, it may lie gently at the foot of peace, and be no further harmful except in appearance."

"Your grace must pardon me," Louis the Dauphin said. "I will not go back to France. I am too highly born to be treated like a piece of property, to be a second-in-command, or a useful serving man and instrument to any sovereign state throughout the world.

"Your breath first enflamed the dead embers of wars between this chastised Kingdom and myself and brought in matter that should feed this fire, and now it is far too huge to be blown out with that same weak wind which inflamed it.

"You taught me how to know the face of right, you acquainted me with my interest in — my valid claim to — this land. Yes, you thrust this enterprise into my heart, and now you come to tell me that King John has made his peace with Rome? What is that peace to me?

"I, by the honor of my marriage bed, after the death of young Arthur, claim this land for mine. As the husband of Blanche, I am next in line to the English throne.

"And, now that England is half-conquered, must I go back to France because King John has made his peace with Rome? Am I Rome's slave? What penny has Rome spent on this military expedition, what men has Rome provided, what munitions has Rome sent to prop up and support this military action? Isn't it I who take on this expense? Who else but I, and such as to my claim are liable, sweat in this business and maintain this war?

"Haven't I heard these islanders shout out, '*Vive le Roi!*' — 'Long live the King! — as I have traveled past their towns? Haven't I here the best cards for the game, to win this easy match played for a crown? And shall I now give up all that has already been conceded to me? This is a game that I have almost won and that I will win.

"No, no, on my soul, it never shall be said that I gave up such an easy victory."

"You look only on the outside of this work," Cardinal Pandulph said. "You are looking only at the surface."

Louis the Dauphin replied, "Outside or inside, I will not return to France until my attempt so much is glorified as was promised to my ample hope before I gathered this gallant army of war, and selected these fiery spirits from the world to stare down conquest and to win renown even in the jaws of danger and of death."

A trumpet sounded to announce an important visitor.

"What robust trumpet thus summons us?" Louis the Dauphin asked.

The Bastard arrived, accompanied by attendants.

"Let me have audience in accordance with the fair play and rules of chivalry of the world," the Bastard said to the Dauphin. "I have been sent to speak to you."

He then said to Cardinal Pandulph, "My holy lord of Milan, I have come from King John to learn how you have done on his behalf. And, as you answer, I know the scope and warrant limited to my tongue. As you answer, I know what I can and I cannot say in my position as King John's ambassador."

Cardinal Pandulph said, "The Dauphin is too obstinately hostile, and he will not conform to my entreaties. He flatly says he'll not lay down his arms."

Referring to young Lewis the Dauphin, the Bastard said, "By all the blood that fury ever breathed, the youth says well."

The Bastard preferred warfare to diplomacy.

He then said to Lewis the Dauphin, "Now hear our English King, for thus his royalty speaks through me.

"He is prepared, as is reasonable he should be prepared.

"King John smiles at this apish and unmannerly approach, this armed masquerade and unadvised revelry, this unbearded sauciness and these boyish troops, and he is well prepared to whip this dwarfish war, these pigmy arms, from out of the circle of his territories.

"Think of that hand which had the strength, even at your door, to cudgel you and make you leap over the bottom half of a two-part stable door, to dive like buckets in concealed wells, to crouch in the straw covering your stable floors, to lie like pawned articles locked up in chests and trunks, to cuddle with swine, to seek sweet safety in vaults and prisons, and to shiver and shake even at the crying of your nation's crow, thinking that the crow's voice comes from an armed Englishman.

"Shall that victorious hand be enfeebled here in England, that victorious hand which in your own chambers in France chastised you?

"No.

"Know the gallant monarch is in arms and like an eagle over his aery soars in order to swoop down on and drive away any annoyance that comes near his nest.

"And you degenerate, you ingrate rebels, you bloody Neroes, ripping up the womb of your dear mother England the way that Emperor Nero of Rome ripped up his mother's womb after he murdered her, blush for shame, for your own ladies and pale-faced maidens like Amazonian warrior-women come tripping after drums, their thimbles changed to armed gauntlets, their needles changed to lances, and their gentle and peaceful hearts changed to fierce and bloody inclination."

Louis the Dauphin said, "There end your bravado, and turn your face away in peace. We grant that you can out-scold us.

"Fare you well. We regard our time as too precious to be spent with such a braggart."

"Give me permission to speak," Cardinal Pandulph said.

"No, I will speak," the Bastard said.

Using the royal plural, Louis the Dauphin said, "We will listen to neither of you."

He ordered, "Strike up the drums, and let the tongue of war plead for our interest and our being here."

The Bastard said, "Indeed your drums, being beaten, will cry out, and so shall you, when you are beaten. Do but start an echo with the clamor of your drum, and even at hand a drum is ready braced that shall reverberate entirely as loudly as your drum. Sound another drum of yours, and another drum of ours shall sound as loud as your drum and rattle the sky's ear and mock the deep-mouthed thunder.

"Now at hand, close by, not trusting to this dilatory, shifting legate here, whom he has used for entertainment rather than need is warlike John, and on his forehead sits a bare-ribbed death — a skeleton — whose duty this day is to feast upon whole thousands of the French."

"Strike up our drums so we can find this danger," Louis the Dauphin said.

"And you shall find it, Dauphin," the Bastard said. "Do not doubt it."

King John and Hubert talked together on the battlefield as the battle raged.

"How goes the day with us?" King John asked. "Who is winning? Tell me, Hubert."

"It goes badly for us, I fear," Hubert replied. "How fares your majesty? How are you?"

"This fever, which has troubled me so long, lies heavy on me," King John said. "My heart is sick!"

A messenger arrived and said, "My lord, your valiant kinsman, Faulconbridge, wants your majesty to leave the battlefield and send him word by me which way you go."

Faulconbridge was Sir Richard, aka the Bastard.

"Tell him that I am going toward Swinstead, to the abbey there," King John said.

"Be of good comfort because the great supply of reinforcement troops that was expected by the Dauphin here was wrecked three nights ago on Goodwin Sands," the messenger said. "This news was brought to Sir Richard just now. The French fight coldly, and they are retreating."

"Ay, me!" King John said. "This tyrant fever burns me up, and it will not let me welcome this good news. Let's set on toward Swinstead. Take me immediately to my litter. Weakness possesses me, and I am faint."

In another part of the battlefield, the Earl of Salisbury, the Earl of Pembroke, and Lord Bigot talked among themselves. Some soldiers were present.

The Earl of Salisbury said, "I did not think that King John had so many friends who were willing to fight for him."

"Let's go and fight once again and put spirit in the French," the Earl of Pembroke said. "If the French are destroyed, we are, too."

"That misbegotten Devil, Faulconbridge, in spite of spite and in defiance of anything we can do, alone upholds the day," the Earl of Salisbury said. "He is holding the English troops together."

"They say King John — who is very sick — has left the battlefield," the Earl of Pembroke said.

Lord Melun, a Frenchman, arrived. He was mortally wounded.

He said, "Lead me to the rebels of England here."

"When we were happy, we had other names," the Earl of Salisbury said.

He disliked being called rebel.

The Earl of Pembroke said, "This man is the Count Melun."

"Wounded to death," the Earl of Salisbury said.

"Flee, noble Englishmen," Lord Melun said. "You are bought and sold; you are betrayed. Unthread the rude eye of rebellion and welcome home again your discarded faith."

Lord Melun was using the metaphor of a needle and thread. The thread of rebellion had been pushed through the eye of the needle, and now Lord Melun wanted the English rebels to pull the thread back out of the eye of the needle. He wanted them to retrace the steps that had taken them through the difficult passage leading to rebellion.

He continued, "Seek out King John and fall before his feet, for if the French become lords of this loud day by winning the battle, Louis the Dauphin intends to recompense the pains you are taking for him by cutting off your heads. Thus has he sworn and I with him, and many more with me, upon the altar at Saint Edmundsbury, even on that altar where we swore to you dear friendship and everlasting love."

"Can this be possible?" the Earl of Salisbury asked. "Can this be true?"

Lord Melun said, "Don't I have hideous death within my view? Don't I retain only a small quantity of life, which bleeds away like a wax figure melting and losing its shape from the heat of a fire?"

Witches were reputed to be able to kill by making and melting wax figures of their enemies.

He continued, "What in the world can make me now deceive, since I must lose the profit of all deceit? Why should I then be false, since it is true that I must die here and live hence by truth?"

To get into Heaven, Lord Melun needed to be truthful here on Earth.

He continued, "I say again, if Louis wins the day's battle, he is forsworn if ever those eyes of yours see another day break in the East. He has sworn that if he wins this battle, you will not live to see another dawn. Instead, this ill night, whose black contagious breath already smokes about the burning crest of the old, feeble, and day-wearied Sun, your breathing shall expire, paying the fine of rated — evaluated — and berated treachery even with a treacherous fine, aka end, of all your lives, if Louis with your assistance wins the day.

"Commend me to a man named Hubert who is with your King John. Because of my friendship with him, and because my grandfather was an Englishman, my conscience has awakened and confessed all this.

"In recompense for this, please carry me away from the noise and tumult of the battlefield to somewhere I may think the remnant of my thoughts in peace, and part this body and my soul with contemplation and devout desires. I want to die in peace."

"We believe what you have confessed to us," the Earl of Salisbury said. "Curse my soul if I do not love the appearance and the manner of this most fair occasion and opportunity, by means of which we will retrace the steps of damned flight, and like an abated and retired flood, leaving our rankness and irregular course, stoop low within those bounds we have overflowed and calmly run on in obedience even to our ocean, to our great King John.

"My arm shall give you, Lord Melun, help to bear you away from here, for I see the cruel pangs of death unmistakably in your eye.

"Let's go, my friends! New flight and happy change maintain old right. We will flee to King John and be loyal again."

Louis the Dauphin and his attendants were in the French camp following the battle.

He said, "I thought that the Sun of Heaven was loath to set; instead, it stayed in the sky and made the western welkin blush when the English traversed backward over their own ground in faint-hearted retreat. Oh, we came splendidly off the battlefield, when with a volley of our unnecessary shot at the retreating enemy, after such bloody toil, we bid them good night. We then wound our waving battle flags up without opposition from the English. We were the last remaining soldiers in the battlefield, and we were almost lords of it!"

A messenger arrived and asked, "Where is my Prince, the Dauphin?"

"Here I am," Louis the Dauphin said. "What is your news?"

The messenger replied, "The Count Melun has been slain; the rebelling English lords by his persuasion have deserted you and returned to King John, and your reinforcements, for whom you have wished so long, have been destroyed and sunk on Goodwin Sands."

"This is foul and ominous news!" Louis the Dauphin said. "Curse your very heart! I did not think to be as sad tonight as this has made me. Who was he who said that King John fled an hour or two before the stumble-causing night parted our weary armies?"

"Whoever spoke it, it is true, my lord," the messenger said.

"Good," Louis the Dauphin said. "Keep good guard and take good care tonight. The Sun shall not be up as soon as I will be to try the fair venture of tomorrow."

In an open space in the neighborhood of Swinstead Abbey, the Bastard and Hubert met. The night was dark, and they did not recognize each other.

"Who's there?" Hubert asked, "Speak! Speak quickly, or I'll shoot."

"I am a friend," the Bastard said. "Who are you?"

"I am on the side of England," Hubert said.

"Where are you going?" the Bastard asked.

"What's that to you?" Hubert asked. "Why can't I ask about your business just like you ask about mine?"

Recognizing his voice, the Bastard said, "You are Hubert, I think."

Hubert replied, "You think correctly. I will bet anything that you are my friend, since you know my voice so well. Who are you?"

"Whoever you want me to be," the Bastard said. "But if you please, you will be my friend if you think I am descended on one side from the Plantagenets."

Knowing that he was talking to Sir Richard, aka the Bastard, Hubert said, "My memory is faulty and unkind! I should have recognized your voice. You and the eyeless night have done me shame — you by recognizing my voice when I did not recognize yours, and the night by keeping me from clearly seeing you and thereby recognizing you.

"Brave soldier, pardon me that any accent breaking from your tongue should escape the true acquaintance of my ear. I apologize for not recognizing your voice."

"Come, come," the Bastard said. "There's no need for apologies. What news is abroad?"

"To bring you the news is my reason for walking here in the black brow of night as I seek to find you."

"Be quick, then," the Bastard said. "What's the news?"

"Oh, my sweet sir, this news is suitable for the night — it is black, fearsome, comfortless, and horrible."

"Show me the very wound of this ill news," the Bastard said. "I am no woman. I'll not swoon when I hear it."

"The King, I am afraid, has been poisoned by a monk," Hubert said. "I left King John almost unable to speak, and I rushed out to inform you of this evil so that you could better arm yourself for the unexpected emergency than if you had after a delay learned about this."

"How was he poisoned?" the Bastard asked. "Who was his food taster?"

A food taster ate a portion of the King's food to check for poison before the King ate.

"A monk," Hubert said. "I must say that he was a determined villain who deliberately ate the poison — as a result, his bowels suddenly exploded.

"King John still speaks and perhaps may recover."

"Who did you leave to tend his majesty?" the Bastard asked.

"Haven't you heard?" Hubert asked. "The rebelling English lords have all come back, and they brought Prince Henry, King John's son — in their company. At Prince Henry's request, the King has pardoned them, and they are all around his majesty."

Referring to the poisoning of King John, the Bastard prayed, "Withhold your indignation, mighty Heaven, and tempt us not to bear above our power! Don't give us more trouble than we can endure."

He then said, "I need to tell you, Hubert, that half my army last night, passing these flatlands, were taken by the tide. These Lincoln Washes have devoured them; they drowned. I myself, well mounted on a good horse, barely and with great difficulty escaped.

"Let's go. Lead the way. Conduct me to King John. I am afraid that he will be dead before I see him."

In the garden of Swinstead Abbey, Prince Henry, the Earl of Salisbury, and Lord Bigot talked.

"It is too late," Prince Henry said. "The life of all his blood is infected and corrupted, and his pure, uncorrupted brain, which some suppose to be the soul's frail dwelling-house, foretells by the foolish, lunatic comments that it makes the ending of mortality. Clearly, my father is dying."

The Earl of Pembroke entered the scene and said, "His highness is still able to speak, and he believes that if he were brought into the open air, it would lessen the burning quality of that deadly poison which assails him."

"Let him be brought into the garden here," Prince Henry ordered.

Lord Bigot exited.

Prince Henry continued, "Does he still rave?"

"He is calmer than when you left him," the Earl of Pembroke said. "Just now he sang."

"Oh, delusion of sickness!" Prince Henry said. "Fierce extremes in their continuance will not feel themselves. As they continue, they will not be felt. Death, having preyed upon the outward parts, leaves them insensible, and his siege is now against the mind, which he pricks and wounds with many legions of strange fantasies, which in a throng press to that last stronghold and confound and destroy themselves — the dying person becomes incoherent.

"It is strange that death should sing. I am the cygnet — baby swan — of this pale, faint swan, who chants a doleful hymn to his own death, and from the organ-pipe of frailty sings his soul and body to their lasting rest."

Swans were thought to sing only when dying.

"Be consoled, Prince," the Earl of Salisbury said, "for you are born to set a form upon that formless mass which he has left so shapeless and so rude. You were born to bring order to the chaos that England currently endures."

Some attendants and Lord Bigot carried King John in a chair over to Prince Henry and the lords.

"Yes, by the Virgin Mary," King John said, "now my soul has elbow-room. It would not go out through windows or through doors. There is so hot a summer in my bosom that all my bowels crumble to dust. I am a scribbled form, drawn with a pen upon a parchment, and against this fire I shrink the way parchment does when it is too close to a fire."

"How fares your majesty?" Prince Henry asked. "How are you?"

"I am poisoned — I fare ill. I fare badly as a result of eating ill fare, aka food. I am dead, forsaken, and cast off, and none of you will bid the winter to come and thrust his icy fingers in my mouth, nor will you let my Kingdom's rivers take their course through my burned bosom, nor will you entreat the north to make its bleak winds kiss my parched lips and comfort me with cold. I do not ask much from you; I beg cold comfort — the comfort that I can get from the cold. But you are so stingy and so ungrateful that you deny me even cold comfort."

Even while dying, King John was capable of punning. Another meaning of "cold comfort" is "little comfort."

"I wish that there were some virtuous, helping quality in my tears, so they might relieve you!" Prince Henry said.

"The salt in them is hot," King John replied.

Tears of grief are hot. Because of the way that King John was dying, anything hot was unpleasant to him. In addition, he was aware of the medical theory that salt is necessary for healthy blood, and he was saying that he was too far gone for the salt in his son's tears to make his blood healthy again.

King John continued, "Within me is a Hell, and there the poison is as a fiend confined to tyrannize on unreprievable, condemned blood."

Sinners were thought to carry Hell within themselves. That King John had a Hell within him may make us doubt that his soul flew upward to Heaven when he died.

"Unreprievable, condemned blood" is like the blood of a criminal who has been condemned to die and who will not be pardoned.

The Bastard entered the scene and said, "I am heated with my intense desire and impetuous speed to see your majesty!"

"Kinsman, you have come to close my eyes after I die," King John said. "The tackle of my heart is cracked and burned, and all the shrouds wherewith my life should sail are turned to one thread, one little hair. My heart has one poor string to support it, one string that will hold only until your news has been uttered, and then all this you see is only a clod of clay and an empty model of destroyed royalty."

This society believed that heartstrings supported the heart; when someone died, their heartstrings broke. King John was saying that he had only one heartstring left to support his heart. He also was comparing heartstrings to the tackle, aka rigging, of a ship, including the shrouds, aka ropes that supported the mast.

King John had asked for the Bastard's news, and so the Bastard told him his news: "The Dauphin is preparing to come here, and only Heaven knows how we shall fight and repel him, for at night the best part of my army, when I took advantage of an opportunity and moved it, was in the Washes all unexpectedly devoured by the unexpected flood. The greater part of my soldiers drowned."

King John died. The new King was his son; Prince Henry now became King Henry III.

The Earl of Salisbury said to the Bastard, "You speak this dead news in as dead an ear."

Dead news is deadly news.

He continued, "My liege! My lord! A moment ago you were a King, and now you are this."

"Even so must I run on, and even so I must stop," King Henry III said. "Like my father the King, I will live, and I will die. What security of the world, what hope, what support can exist when this was just now a King, and is now clay?"

"Are you gone so?" the Bastard said to King John's corpse. "I stay behind only to do the duty of revenge for you, and then my soul shall attend on you in Heaven, as my soul on Earth has always been your servant."

He said to the lords who had rebelled but then had returned to serve King John, "Now, now, you stars who move in your right spheres, where are your powers? Show now your mended faiths, and immediately return with me again to the battlefield to push destruction and perpetual shame out of the weak door of our fainting land. Straightaway let us seek, or straightaway we shall be sought. The Dauphin rages at our very heels. We must fight him."

"It seems then that you don't know what we know," the Earl of Salisbury said. "The Cardinal Pandulph is resting inside. Half an hour ago he came from Louis the Dauphin, and he brought from him such offers of peace as we may accept with honor and respect. Louis the Dauphin intends immediately to stop this war and return to France."

"He will do that when he sees ourselves well prepared to defend ourselves," the Bastard said.

"No," the Earl of Salisbury said. "It is in a way done already, for many cannon and much other military equipment he has sent to the seaside, and he has put his cause and quarrel to the disposition of Cardinal Pandulph, with whom you, myself, and other lords, if you think it is suitable, this afternoon will go to consummate this business happily."

"Let it be done," the Bastard said, "and you, my noble Prince, with other nobles who may best be spared, shall attend your father's funeral."

King Henry III said, "At Worcester his body must be interred, for so he willed it."

"And so it shall be then," the Bastard said, "and happily may your sweet self put on the lineal state and glory of the land! To you with all submission and on my knee, I bequeath my faithful services and true subjection everlastingly."

The Bastard and the other lords knelt as they pledged to be loyal to the new King of England.

The Earl of Salisbury said, "And the same offer of our love we make, to continue without a stain of disloyalty for evermore."

King Henry III said, "I have a kind soul that would give you thanks and knows not how to do it except with tears."

The Bastard and the other lords rose.

"Let us pay the time only necessary woe," the Bastard said, "since it has been beforehand with our griefs."

Their griefs, in part, had already been remedied. King John had died, but King Edward III had taken his place. England had been at war with France, but now that war had ended.

The Bastard continued, "This England never did, and never shall, lie at the proud foot of a conqueror, except when it first helped to wound itself with disloyalty. Now that these her lords have come home and are loyal again, let the three remaining corners of the world come against us in arms, and we shall forcibly repel them. Nothing shall make us rue, if England to itself do remain but true."

Appendix A: Brief Historical Background

KING RICHARD I: 1189-1199

He was also known as Richard the Lionheart because of his military prowess as a leader and soldier. He was a Christian commander in the Third Crusade. As King, he spent little time in England. Much of his time was spent defending his lands in France. He also spent time in captivity.

KING JOHN: 1199-1216

He was also known as John Lackland because he lost the Duchy of Normandy and most of his lands in France. In 1215, he signed the Magna Carta. King John is a bad king in Robin Hood stories.

KING HENRY III: 1216-1272

Son of King John, he reigned for 56 years. At the beginning of his reign, much of England was controlled by the French Prince Louis (later King Louis VIII), but at the end of his reign, England was controlled by the King of England.

KING EDWARD I: 1272-1307

Edward Longshanks fought and defeated the Welsh chieftains, and he made his eldest son the Prince of Wales. He won victories against the Scots, and he brought the coronation stone from Scone to Westminster.

KING EDWARD II: 1307-deposed 1327

At the Battle of Bannockburn in 1314, the Scots defeated his army. His wife and her lover, Mortimer, deposed him. According to legend, he was murdered in Berkeley Castle by means of a red-hot poker thrust up his anus.

KING EDWARD III: 1327-1377

Son of King Edward II, he reigned for a long time — 50 years. Because he wanted to conquer Scotland and France, he started the Hundred Years War in 1338. King Edward III and his eldest son, Edward the Black Prince, won important victories Battle of Poitiers (1356).

One of King Edward III's sons was John of Gaunt, first Duke of Lancaster.

Another of King Edward against the French in the Battle of Crécy (1346) and the

III's sons was Edmund of Langley, first Duke of York.

During his reign, the Black Death — the bubonic plague — struck in 1348-1350 and killed half of England's population.

KING RICHARD II: 1377-deposed 1399

King Richard II was the son of Edward the Black Prince. In 1381, Wat Tyler led the Peasants Revolt, which was suppressed. King Richard II sent Henry, Duke of Lancaster, into exile and seized Henry's estates, but in 1399 Henry, Duke of Lancaster, returned from exile and deposed King Richard II, thereby becoming King Henry IV. In 1400, King Richard II was murdered in Pontefract Castle, which is also known as Pomfret Castle.

HOUSE OF LANCASTER

KING HENRY IV: 1399-1413

Henry, Duke of Lancaster, was the son of John of Gaunt, who was the third son of King Edward III. He was born at Bolingbroke Castle and so was also known as Henry of Bolingbroke. Returning from exile in France to reclaim his estates, he deposed King Richard II. He spent the 13 years of his reign putting down rebellions and defending himself against those who would assassinate or depose him. The Welshman Owen Glendower and the English Percy family were among those who fought against him. King Henry IV died at the age of 45.

KING HENRY V: 1413-1422

The son of King Henry IV, King Henry V renewed the war with France. He and his army defeated the French at the Battle of Agincourt (1415) despite being heavily outnumbered. He married Catherine of Valoise, the daughter of the French King, but he died before becoming King of France. He left behind a 10-month-old son, who became King Henry VI.

KING HENRY VI: 1422-deposed 1461; briefly returned to the throne in 1470-1471

The Hundred Years War ended in 1453; the English lost all land in France except for Calais, a port city. After King Henry VI suffered an attack of mental illness in 1454, Richard, third Duke of York and the father of King Henry IV and King Richard III, was made Protector of the Realm. England suffered civil war after the House of York challenged King Henry VI's right to be King of England. In 1470, King Henry VI was briefly restored to the English throne. In 1471, he was murdered in the Tower of London. A short time previously, his son, Edward, Prince of Wales, had been killed at the Battle of Tewkesbury in 1471; this was the final battle in the Wars of the Roses. The Yorkists decisively defeated the Lancastrians.

King Henry VI founded both Eton College and King's College, Cambridge.

WARS OF THE ROSES

From 1455-1487, the Yorkists and the Lancastrians fought for power in England in the famous Wars of the Roses. The emblem of the York family was a white rose, and the emblem of the Lancaster family was a red rose. The Yorkists and the Lancastrians were descended from King Edward III.

HOUSE OF YORK

KING EDWARD IV: 1461-1483 (King Henry VI briefly returned to the throne in 1470-1471)

Son of Richard, third Duke of York, he charged his brother George, Duke of Clarence, with treason and had him murdered in 1478. After dying suddenly, he left behind two sons aged 12 and 9, and five daughters.

His surviving two brothers in Shakespeare's play *Richard III* are these: 1) George, Duke of Clarence. Clarence is the second-oldest brother; and 2) Richard, Duke of Gloucester, and afterwards King Richard III. Gloucester is the youngest surviving brother.

William Caxton established the first printing press in Westminster during King Edward IV's reign.

KING EDWARD V: 1483-1483

The eldest son of King Edward IV, he reigned for only two months, the shortest-lived monarch in English history. He was 13 years old. He and his younger brother, Richard, were murdered in the Tower of London. According to Shakespeare's play, their uncle, Richard, Duke of Gloucester, who became King Richard III, was responsible for their murders.

KING RICHARD III: 1483-1485

Brother of King Edward IV, Richard, the Duke of Gloucester, declared the two Princes in the Tower of London — King Edward V and Richard, Duke of York — illegitimate and made himself King Richard III. In 1485, Henry Tudor, Earl of Richmond, a descendant of John of Gaunt, who was the father of King Henry IV, defeated King Richard III at the Battle of Bosworth Field in Leicestershire. King Richard III died in that battle.

King Richard III's father was Richard Plantagenet, Duke of York. His mother was Cecily Neville, Duchess of York.

King Richard III's death in the Battle of Bosworth Field is regarded as marking the end of the Middle Ages in England.

A NOTE ON THE PLANTAGENETS

The first Plantagenet King was King Henry II (1154-1189). From 1154 until 1485, when King Richard III died, all English Kings were Plantagenets. Both the Lancaster family and the York family were Plantagenets.

Geoffrey Plantagenet, Count of Anjou, was the founder of the House of Plantagenet. Geoffrey's son, Henry Curtmantle, became King Henry II of England, thereby founding the Plantagenet dynasty. Geoffrey wore a sprig of broom, a flowering shrub, as a badge; the Latin name for broom is *planta genista*, and from it the name "Plantagenet" arose.

The Plantagenet dynasty can be divided into three parts:

1154-1216: The Angevins. The Angevin Kings were Henry II, Richard I (Richard the Lionheart), and John 1.

1216-1399: The Plantagenets. These Kings ranged from King Henry III to King Richard II.

1399-1485: The Houses of Lancaster and of York. These Kings ranged from King Henry IV to King Richard III.

BEGINNING OF THE TUDOR DYNASTY

KING HENRY VII: 1485-1509

When King Richard III fell at the Battle of Bosworth, Henry Tudor, Earl of Richmond, became King Henry VII. A Lancastrian, he married Elizabeth of York — young Elizabeth of York in *Richard III* — and united the two warring houses, York and Lancaster, thus ending the Wars of the Roses. One of his grandfathers was Sir Owen Tudor, who married Catherine of Valoise, widow of King Henry V.

KING HENRY VIII: 1509-1547

King Henry VIII had six wives. These are their fates: "Divorced, Beheaded, Died, Divorced, Beheaded, Survived." He divorced his first wife, Catherine of Aragon, so that he could marry Anne Boleyn. Because of this, England divorced itself from the Catholic Church, and King Henry VIII became the head of the Church of England. King Henry VIII had one son and two daughters, all of whom became rulers of England: Edward, daughter of Jane Seymour; Mary, daughter of Catherine of Aragon; and Elizabeth, daughter of Anne Boleyn.

KING EDWARD VI: 1547-1553

The son of Henry VIII and Jane Seymour, King Edward VI succeeded his father at the age of nine; a Council of Regency with his uncle, Duke of Somerset, styled Protector, ruled the government.

During King Edward VI's reign, Archbishop Thomas Cranmer wrote the 1549 Book of Common Prayer.

When King Edward VI died, Lady Jane Grey was proclaimed Queen, but she ruled for only nine days before being executed in 1554, aged 17. Mary, daughter of Catherine of Aragon, became Queen. She was Catholic, thus the attempt to make Lady Jane Grey, a Protestant, Queen.

QUEEN MARY I (BLOODY MARY) 1553-1558

Queen Mary I attempted to make England a Catholic nation again. Some Protestant bishops, including Archbishop Thomas Cranmer, were burnt at the stake, and other violence broke out, resulting in her being known as Bloody Mary.

QUEEN ELIZABETH I: 1558-1603

The daughter of King Henry VIII and Anne Boleyn, Queen Elizabeth I was a popular Queen. In 1588, the English navy decisively defeated the Spanish Armada. England had many notable playwrights and poets, including William Shakespeare and Ben Jonson, during her reign. She never married and had no children.

KING JAMES I OF ENGLAND: A MEMBER OF THE HOUSE OF STUART

KING JAMES I OF ENGLAND AND VI OF SCOTLAND: 1603-1625

King James I of England was the son of Mary, Queen of Scots, and Lord Darnley. In 1605 Guy Fawkes and his Catholic co-conspirators were captured before they could blow up the Houses of Parliament; this was known as the Gunpowder Plot.

In 1611, during King James I's reign, the Authorized Version of the Bible (the King James Version) was completed.

Also during King James I's reign, in 1620 the Pilgrims sailed for America in their ship *The Mayflower*.

A NOTE ON SHAKESPEARE

William Shakespeare lived under two monarchs: Queen Elizabeth I and King James I.

Appendix B: About the Author

It was a dark and stormy night. Suddenly a cry rang out, and on a hot summer night in 1954, Josephine, wife of Carl Bruce, gave birth to a boy — me. Unfortunately, this young married couple allowed Reuben Saturday, Josephine's brother, to name their first-born. Reuben, aka "The Joker," decided that Bruce was a nice name, so he decided to name me Bruce Bruce. I have gone by my middle name — David — ever since.

Being named Bruce David Bruce hasn't been all bad. Bank tellers remember me very quickly, so I don't often have to show an ID. It can be fun in charades, also. When I was a counselor as a teenager at Camp Echoing Hills in Warsaw, Ohio, a fellow counselor gave the signs for "sounds like" and "two words," then she pointed to a bruise on her leg twice. Bruise Bruise? Oh yeah, Bruce Bruce is the answer!

Uncle Reuben, by the way, gave me a haircut when I was in kindergarten. He cut my hair short and shaved a small bald spot on the back of my head. My mother wouldn't let me go to school until the bald spot grew out again.

Of all my brothers and sisters (six in all), I am the only transplant to Athens, Ohio. I was born in Newark, Ohio, and have lived all around Southeastern Ohio. However, I moved to Athens to go to Ohio University and have never left.

At Ohio U, I never could make up my mind whether to major in English or Philosophy, so I got a bachelor's degree with a double major in both areas, then I added a master's degree in English and a master's degree in Philosophy.

Currently, and for a long time to come (I eat fruits and veggies), I am spending my retirement writing books such as *Nadia Comaneci: Perfect 10*, *The Funniest People in Dance*, *Homer's* Iliad: *A Retelling in Prose*, and *William Shakespeare's* Othello: *A Retelling in Prose*.

By the way, my sister Brenda Kennedy writes romances such as *A New Beginning* and *Shattered Dreams*.

Appendix C: Some Books by David Bruce

Retellings of a Classic Work of Literature

Arden of Faversham: *A Retelling*

Ben Jonson's The Alchemist: *A Retelling*

Ben Jonson's The Arraignment, or Poetaster: *A Retelling*

Ben Jonson's Bartholomew Fair: *A Retelling*

Ben Jonson's The Case is Altered: *A Retelling*

Ben Jonson's Catiline's Conspiracy: *A Retelling*

Ben Jonson's The Devil is an Ass: *A Retelling*

Ben Jonson's Epicene: *A Retelling*

Ben Jonson's Every Man in His Humor: *A Retelling*

Ben Jonson's Every Man Out of His Humor: *A Retelling*

Ben Jonson's The Fountain of Self-Love, or Cynthia's Revels: *A Retelling*

Ben Jonson's The Magnetic Lady, or Humors Reconciled: *A Retelling*

Ben Jonson's The New Inn, or The Light Heart: *A Retelling*

Ben Jonson's Sejanus' Fall: *A Retelling*

Ben Jonson's The Staple of News: *A Retelling*

Ben Jonson's A Tale of a Tub: *A Retelling*

Ben Jonson's Volpone, or the Fox: *A Retelling*

Christopher Marlowe's Complete Plays: Retellings

Christopher Marlowe's Dido, Queen of Carthage: *A Retelling*

Christopher Marlowe's Doctor Faustus: *Retellings of the 1604 A-Text and of the 1616 B-Text*

Christopher Marlowe's Edward II: *A Retelling*

Christopher Marlowe's The Massacre at Paris: *A Retelling*

Christopher Marlowe's The Rich Jew of Malta: *A Retelling*

Christopher Marlowe's Tamburlaine, Parts 1 and 2: *Retellings*

Dante's Divine Comedy: *A Retelling in Prose*

Dante's Inferno: *A Retelling in Prose*

Dante's Purgatory: *A Retelling in Prose*

Dante's Paradise: *A Retelling in Prose*

The Famous Victories of Henry V: *A Retelling*

From the Iliad *to the* Odyssey: *A Retelling in Prose of Quintus of Smyrna's* Posthomerica

George Chapman, Ben Jonson, and John Marston's Eastward Ho! *A Retelling*

George Peele's The Arraignment of Paris: *A Retelling*

George Peele's The Battle of Alcazar: *A Retelling*

George Peele's David and Bathsheba, and the Tragedy of Absalom: *A Retelling*

George Peele's Edward I: *A Retelling*

George Peele's The Old Wives' Tale: *A Retelling*

George-a-Greene: *A Retelling*

The History of King Leir: A Retelling

Homer's Iliad: *A Retelling in Prose*

Homer's Odyssey: *A Retelling in Prose*

J.W. Gent.'s The Valiant Scot: *A Retelling*

Jason and the Argonauts: A Retelling in Prose of Apollonius of Rhodes' Argonautica

John Ford: Eight Plays Translated into Modern English

John Ford's The Broken Heart: *A Retelling*

John Ford's The Fancies, Chaste and Noble: *A Retelling*

John Ford's The Lady's Trial: *A Retelling*

John Ford's The Lover's Melancholy: *A Retelling*

John Ford's Love's Sacrifice: *A Retelling*

John Ford's Perkin Warbeck: *A Retelling*

John Ford's The Queen: *A Retelling*

John Ford's 'Tis Pity She's a Whore: *A Retelling*

John Lyly's Campaspe: *A Retelling*

John Lyly's Endymion, The Man in the Moon: *A Retelling*

John Lyly's Galatea: *A Retelling*

John Lyly's Love's Metamorphosis: *A Retelling*

John Lyly's Midas: *A Retelling*

John Lyly's Mother Bombie: *A Retelling*

John Lyly's Sappho and Phao: *A Retelling*

John Lyly's The Woman in the Moon: *A Retelling*

John Webster's The White Devil: *A Retelling*

King Edward III: *A Retelling*

Mankind: *A Medieval Morality Play* (A Retelling)

Margaret Cavendish's The Unnatural Tragedy: *A Retelling*

The Merry Devil of Edmonton: *A Retelling*

The Summoning of Everyman: *A Medieval Morality Play* (A Retelling)

Robert Greene's Friar Bacon and Friar Bungay: *A Retelling*

The Taming of a Shrew: *A Retelling*

Tarlton's Jests: A Retelling

Thomas Middleton's A Chaste Maid in Cheapside: *A Retelling*

Thomas Middleton's Women Beware Women: *A Retelling*

Thomas Middleton and Thomas Dekker's The Roaring Girl: *A Retelling*

Thomas Middleton and William Rowley's The Changeling: *A Retelling*

The Trojan War and Its Aftermath: Four Ancient Epic Poems

Virgil's Aeneid: *A Retelling in Prose*

William Shakespeare's 5 Late Romances: Retellings in Prose

William Shakespeare's 10 Histories: Retellings in Prose

William Shakespeare's 11 Tragedies: Retellings in Prose

William Shakespeare's 12 Comedies: Retellings in Prose

William Shakespeare's 38 Plays: Retellings in Prose

William Shakespeare's 1 Henry IV, aka Henry IV, Part 1: *A Retelling in Prose*

William Shakespeare's 2 Henry IV, aka Henry IV, Part 2: *A Retelling in Prose*

William Shakespeare's 1 Henry VI, aka Henry VI, Part 1: *A Retelling in Prose*

William Shakespeare's 2 Henry VI, aka Henry VI, Part 2: *A Retelling in Prose*

William Shakespeare's 3 Henry VI, aka Henry VI, Part 3: *A Retelling in Prose*

William Shakespeare's All's Well that Ends Well: *A Retelling in Prose*

William Shakespeare's Antony and Cleopatra: *A Retelling in Prose*

William Shakespeare's As You Like It: *A Retelling in Prose*

William Shakespeare's The Comedy of Errors: *A Retelling in Prose*

William Shakespeare's Coriolanus: *A Retelling in Prose*

William Shakespeare's Cymbeline: *A Retelling in Prose*

William Shakespeare's Hamlet: *A Retelling in Prose*

William Shakespeare's Henry V: *A Retelling in Prose*

William Shakespeare's Henry VIII: *A Retelling in Prose*

William Shakespeare's Julius Caesar: *A Retelling in Prose*

William Shakespeare's King John: *A Retelling in Prose*

William Shakespeare's King Lear: *A Retelling in Prose*

William Shakespeare's Love's Labor's Lost: *A Retelling in Prose*

William Shakespeare's Macbeth: *A Retelling in Prose*

William Shakespeare's Measure for Measure: *A Retelling in Prose*

William Shakespeare's The Merchant of Venice: *A Retelling in Prose*

William Shakespeare's The Merry Wives of Windsor: *A Retelling in Prose*

William Shakespeare's A Midsummer Night's Dream: *A Retelling in Prose*

William Shakespeare's Much Ado About Nothing: *A Retelling in Prose*

William Shakespeare's Othello: *A Retelling in Prose*

William Shakespeare's Pericles, Prince of Tyre: *A Retelling in Prose*

William Shakespeare's Richard II: *A Retelling in Prose*

William Shakespeare's Richard III: *A Retelling in Prose*

William Shakespeare's Romeo and Juliet: *A Retelling in Prose*

William Shakespeare's The Taming of the Shrew: *A Retelling in Prose*

William Shakespeare's The Tempest: *A Retelling in Prose*

William Shakespeare's Timon of Athens: *A Retelling in Prose*

William Shakespeare's Titus Andronicus: *A Retelling in Prose*

William Shakespeare's Troilus and Cressida: *A Retelling in Prose*

William Shakespeare's Twelfth Night: *A Retelling in Prose*

William Shakespeare's The Two Gentlemen of Verona: *A Retelling in Prose*

William Shakespeare's The Two Noble Kinsmen: *A Retelling in Prose*

William Shakespeare's The Winter's Tale: *A Retelling in Prose*